Literary Trail
of Greater Boston

Literary Trail
of Greater Boston

Susan Wilson

for The Boston History Collaborative

Houghton Mifflin Company

Boston • New York

All I need to know I learned from you.

Contents

∽

Acknowledgments

❧

From 1997 through 1999, I was honored to take part in meetings of the Boston History Collaborative, especially those related to the new *Literary Trail of Greater Boston*. Having been intimately involved in the recent development of two of Boston's classic history walks — the Freedom Trail and the Boston Women's Heritage Trail — I was thrilled to listen to ideas about the Literary Trail emerge, grow, and take shape through group discussion and to add my own experiences whenever possible. Without Bob Krim, the director of the Boston History Collaborative, and Lisa Simpson, the director of the Literary Trail (whom I first encountered when she was the director of Orchard House) this book would not have been possible.

While we were developing the pamphlet prototype of this Literary Trail guidebook, there was no one so helpful, wise, and willing as Jayne Gordon, a museum educator and consummate tour guide. The staff at all the original sites — the Omni Parker House, Boston Athenaeum, Gibson House, Boston Public Library, Longfellow National Historic Site, Concord Museum, The Wayside, Orchard House, and The Old Manse — as well as the pamphlet coordinator, Judith Rosen, provided critical support, archival resources, editing skills, and other information.

At Houghton Mifflin, Terry Heagney, Wendy Strothman, Rebecca Saikia-Wilson, Frances Tenenbaum, Julie Burns, and Luise Erdmann enabled me to expand that original pamphlet into this substantially larger book. In the process of adding new sites, new stories, and new characters to the original trail, a number of people proved vitally important. I owe profuse thanks to Mary Frances O'Brien, Bill Grealish, Aaron Schmidt, and Mary Beth Dunhouse of the Boston Public Library; Peter Drummey of the Massachusetts Historical Society; Marvin Hightower of Harvard University; Janet Heywood of Mount Auburn Cemetery; Julie Burba of the Bunting Fellowship of Radcliffe Institute; Kathy Kraft and Marie-Hélène Gold of the Radcliffe Archives; Jean Gibran and my other colleagues on the board of the Boston Women's Heritage Trail; Arthur Marx of the Kennedy School of Government; and Ann Wadsworth of the Boston Athenaeum.

Special thanks to the award-winning writers, all of whom work or live in the Greater Boston area, who agreed to share their words and inspiration in this volume: Anne Bernays, Julia Child, Henry Louis Gates, Jr., Gish Jen, Justin Kaplan, Jane Langton, David McCullough, Robert Pinsky, and Patricia Smith. Finally, my deepest appreciation to those who willingly read and commented on the manuscript in its final stages: Suzy Becker, Anne Bernays, Jane Dawson, Jayne Gordon, Bert Hirshberg, Bob Krim, Askold Melnyczuk, and Lisa Simpson.

Susan Wilson
Cambridge, Massachusetts
November 1999

Introduction

*A*S A SHOWCASE FOR the American Revolution, Boston has long been an unparalleled national treasure. Still, 1776 was not the only important date in American history, and native Bostonians like Paul Revere, John Hancock, and Samuel Adams were not its only heroes.

In the century following America's War for Independence, the Greater Boston area experienced a whole new "revolution" and fostered a whole new image — that of cultural center, intellectual hub, and literary mecca. The great arc linking Boston, Cambridge, and Concord, Massachusetts, was the spawning ground for an astonishing number of innovative thinkers, writers, poets, and social activists, whose interests ranged from transcendentalism and abolitionism to women's rights and spiritual enlightenment. Among the heroes of this era were such household names as Louisa May Alcott, Henry David Thoreau, Henry Wadsworth Longfellow, Harriet Beecher Stowe, Ralph Waldo Emerson, William Lloyd Garrison, Nathaniel Hawthorne, and Julia Ward Howe. They came to join a pantheon of native scribes that began with colonial talents like Cotton Mather, Benjamin Franklin, and Phillis Wheatley and eventually grew to include such contemporary giants as Kahlil Gibran, Willa Cather, Sylvia Plath, Robert Frost, Eugene O'Neill, John Updike, and Doris Kearns Goodwin.

Today, the vibrant literary and political reawakening of nineteenth-century Boston is alive, well, and wonderfully retold along the Literary Trail of Greater Boston. Like the famous Freedom Trail, the Literary Trail links a variety of historic sites. While the Freedom Trail is a walking tour of American Revolutionary landmarks in downtown Boston, the Literary Trail is a lengthier excursion — easy to walk in some areas and, in others, better done by bus, auto, or "T" — connecting homes, gathering places, and landscapes associated with nineteenth-century authors and spotlighting Greater Boston's ongoing leadership in America's literary renaissance.

The trail, which includes sites like the Boston Athenaeum, the Longfellow House in Cambridge, and Orchard House in Concord, will place some of America's most beloved authors in the rich, fascinating context of their times. Visitors will come to know not only their books — America's classiest and most enduring classics — but also the bookstores, lectures, and poetry readings that flourish in Boston today.

The Literary Trail: An Overview

‿

THE MAIN ROUTE OF the Literary Trail is a linear, sometimes winding, journey that begins in downtown Boston, continues through Cambridge, then moves out to Concord. It can be taken as a driving tour at your own pace or on scheduled Literary Trail buses. Each of the three towns can also be toured separately by car, foot, and public transportation.

Interspersed throughout this text are several tours called "Off the Beaten Path." These neighborhood walks lead visitors through specific areas adjacent to the main route of the Literary Trail. Because of the one-way streets, heavy traffic, or the difficulty of parking near many of the sites, these are best done on foot. Again, each excursion can be taken on its own or as part of a full day of literary touring.

Since many of the sites are privately owned, please respect the properties and their residents. Many sites are open to the public for free or nominal admissions. A list at the end of this book provides complete information on these sites.

Also scattered throughout the text are segments called "Author/ Author!" Though we wanted to include contemporary authors in Boston, Cambridge, and Concord, it's likely that few would be pleased if visitors stopped by their homes. So we asked several of the area's writers to create short pieces about their local inspirations. In prose and poem, they responded with wonderful insights and anecdotes about themselves and on the literary people and places of Greater Boston that had moved their hearts and minds.

Boston

⤳

THE CITY OF BOSTON, established by British colonists in 1630, has long been credited as the Cradle of Liberty and the Birthplace of the American Revolution.

Less than a century after our War for Independence, however, its image had changed considerably: by then a large, bustling urban center, nineteenth-century Boston became as heralded for its wealth, wit, and wisdom as it had been for its revolutionary roots.

The social and cultural progress of these former Puritans could be seen in a variety of ways. It included social activism, especially in the areas of abolitionism and women's rights, a religious reawakening and renewed love of nature that merged into indigenous new philosophies like transcendentalism, and a literary Golden Age that nurtured many of the nation's first significant writers, poets, and philosophers as well as publishing houses, periodicals, bookstores, and libraries.

Two of Boston's most enduring nicknames — the Athens of America and the Hub of the Solar System — were direct references to this Golden Age of the mid-1800s, when the city held a preeminent position in literature and the arts. Athens, after all, had been the ancient hub of classical culture and learning. Now Boston was laying its own claim to being the New World's Hub — a center of creativity around which Nathaniel Hawthorne, Henry Wadsworth Longfellow, Louisa May Alcott, Harriet Beecher Stowe, Ralph Waldo Emerson, and other notable literati swarmed like so many illustrious bees.

The Boston Literary Trail begins at the **Omni Parker House,** on the corner of School and Tremont streets. Renowned as the oldest continuously operating hotel in America, the hotel and its restaurants have been credited with a bevy of famous firsts, including the Parker House Roll, Boston Cream Pie, and the term "scrod." It was also known for being the first Boston hotel to offer hot and cold running water in the rooms and the first to import a French chef, who was paid the unprecedented

Downtown Boston Tour

1 Omni Parker House hotel
2 Site of America's First Public School
  Old City Hall
3 Old Corner Book Store building
4 Old South Meeting House
5 Site of Elizabeth Peabody Book Shop
6 Site of Newspaper Row, Pi Alley
7 Site of New-England Courant building
8 King's Chapel Burying Ground
9 Tremont Temple
10 Granary Burying Ground

11 Park Street Church
12 Park Street Station
13 Amory-Ticknor house
14 Boston Athenaeum
15 Former Bellevue Hotel
16 Robert Gould Shaw/54th Regiment
  Memorial
17 Massachusetts State House
18 Boston Common
19 Site of Edgar Allan Poe lodgings
20 Colonial Theater

Parker House, circa 1860s

salary of $8,000 a year in the 1850s. Though the elegant old inn has hosted, toasted, or employed numerous celebrities over the decades — from John Wilkes Booth, Charlotte Cushman, Ulysses S. Grant, Ho Chi Minh, and Elizabeth Cady Stanton to Joan Crawford, John F. Kennedy, Malcolm X, Babe Ruth, and Martin Luther King, Jr. — its most famous group of patrons were the members of the **Saturday Club.**

Beginning in the mid-1850s, a select group of talented men assembled at the old Parker House (which the current Parker House replaced in 1927) on the last Saturday afternoon of each month. Their notoriously festive roundtables featured readings and intellectual exchanges amid endlessly flowing chatter, mirth, food, and spirits. Among the members were the philosopher Ralph Waldo Emerson, James Russell Lowell, a poet and editor of the *Atlantic Monthly,* the novelist Nathaniel Hawthorne, the poets John Greenleaf Whittier and Henry Wadsworth Longfellow, and "the autocrat of the breakfast table," Oliver Wendell Holmes.

International literary stars like Britain's **Charles Dickens** (1812– 1870) also dropped by for stimulating afternoons with these Parker House patrons. In an 1867 letter to his daughter, Dickens gushed about the marvels of Boston's finest new hotel: *This is an immense hotel, with all manner of white marble public passages and public rooms. I live in a corner, high up, and have a hot and cold bath in my bedroom (connecting with the sitting room) and comforts not in existence when I was here before. The cost of living is enormous, but*

Charles Dickens

happily we can afford it. I dine to-day with Longfel-low, Emerson, Holmes, and Agassiz. Longfellow was here yesterday. Perfectly white in hair and beard, but a remarkably handsome and notable-looking man.

Turn half-way round, and let your look survey
The white façade that gleams across the way, —
The many-windowed building, tall and wide,
The palace-inn that shows its northern side . . .
Such feasts! The laughs of many a jocund hour
That shook the mortar from King George's tower;
Such guests! What famous names its record boasts,
Whose owners wander in the mob of ghosts!

— Oliver Wendell Holmes,
"At the Saturday Club"

Dickens's presence in Boston always created a stir. When staying at Parker's, he took lengthy walks almost every afternoon, dressed flamboyantly in a brightly colored coat and shiny boots, accessorized with a striped cravat, fine hat, and gloves. Guards were regularly assigned to his hotel room door, since curious fans were eager to watch him rehearsing the exaggerated gestures and odd facial expressions he used to create characters in his animated public readings.

Animation also got Dickens in trouble one festive night, as remembered by Annie Fields in *Memories of a Hostess* (1922): *After the dinner (at the Parker) the other night, Mr. Dickens thought he would take a warm bath; but, the water being drawn, he began playing the clown in pantomime on the edge of the bath (with his clothes on) . . . [I]n a moment, and before he knew where he was, he had tumbled in head over heels, clothes and all.*

This wealth of prestigious clients ensured the Parker House a prominent place in literary history: here Dickens gave his first American reading of "A Christmas Carol" before presenting it to audiences at the Tremont Theater nearby; here Longfellow drafted "Paul Revere's Ride," and here the idea for the *Atlantic Monthly* was born.

Visitors to the Omni Parker House can still see the fireplace mantel from Dickens's room and the mirror he used when practicing his gestures. You can also enjoy Parker's Bar, where the Saturday Club met, as well as the Press Room, where John F. Kennedy announced his bid for Congress in 1946.

Too far afield to be on the Literary Trail is the **John F. Kennedy Library and Museum.** Opened in 1979 near the campus of the University of Massachusetts at Columbia Point, the library holds many treasures connected with the

Bay State's political son, who won the Pulitzer Prize in 1957 for *Profiles in Courage*. A literary bonus is the library's collection of Ernest Hemingway's books, papers, and memorabilia, donated by his widow, Mary Hemingway.

Another significant site that's off the trail is the home of **Malcolm X** (1925–1965), on Dale Street in Roxbury. Born in Omaha, Malcolm Little spent his formative years in Boston. In the period immediately preceding America's entrance into World War II, Malcolm was a busboy at the Parker House. Scarred by a difficult childhood — his father was murdered and his mother institutionalized — Malcolm quickly entered a life of crime, ending up in the Charlestown (Mass.) State Prison. Here he

Malcolm X

discovered the Black Muslim faith, which changed his life.

In *The Autobiography of Malcolm X* (1965), written with Alex Haley, the radical black leader credited the Hub with his conversion and salvation: *All praise is due to Allah that I moved to Boston when I did. If I hadn't, I'd probably still be a brain-washed black Christian.*

Across from the School Street entrance to the Omni Parker House, embedded in the sidewalk, is a folk art mosaic by Lilli Ann Killen Rosenberg. This spot behind the rough granite exterior of King's Chapel was the site of **America's first public school,** the precursor of the Boston Latin School. Among its graduates were Ralph Waldo Emerson, Cotton Mather, Edward Everett Hale, John Hancock, Samuel Adams, William Ellery Channing, Henry Ward Beecher, Francis Parkman, and James Freeman Clarke. Its most famous dropout was Benjamin Franklin.

Though he left the school, the versatile Franklin is still hovering nearby. In the courtyard behind the Latin School site, a larger-than-life bronze statue of a mature Franklin shares the space with Josiah Quincy. When Richard Saltonstall Greenough was sculpting the realistic image, he copied one of Franklin's fur-trimmed suits, now owned by the Massachusetts

BOSTON CITY HALL

was built in 1865. On this site was located the first public school in America. There is an annex at the rear of the building.

Postcard of Old Boston City Hall, ca. 1912

connection, he clearly modeled *The Last Hurrah*'s Frank Skeffington, Jr., after Curley and his city hall after what he called this "lunatic pile of a building: a great, grim, resolutely ugly dustcatcher."

While working at Old City Hall or at the State House up the street, Curley — a roguish Irish-American politician of limited morality and unlimited charm — presided over important luncheons in the main dining room of the Parker

Historical Society. The 1856 sculpture was the first statue of a public person erected in Boston. Josiah Quincy, whose statue was designed by Thomas Ball in 1879, was a president of Harvard College as well as a writer and lawyer and one of three Josiah Quincys to serve as mayor of Boston during the nineteenth century.

The large ornate structure looming over Franklin, Quincy, and the courtyard is **Old City Hall**, whose most colorful occupant was yet another Boston mayor, James Michael Curley. Both the structure and the mayor played a large part in *The Last Hurrah* (1956). Its author, **Edwin O'Connor** (1918–1968), began his professional career as a radio announcer and producer and a reviewer for the *Boston Herald*. Still, he will always be remembered for his fiction. His novel *The Edge of Sadness* won the Pulitzer Prize in 1961.

Though O'Connor denied the

Last Hurrah movie still with Spencer Tracy

I'm not just an elected official of the city; I'm a tribal chieftain as well.

— Frank Skeffington, Jr., in *The Last Hurrah* (1956)

House. It's no coincidence that "The Last Hurrah" is the name of a bar in the Omni Parker House.

Curley's life and character have intrigued many writers and inspired many books, from Joseph Dineen's *The Purple Shamrock* (1949) to James Carroll's *Mortal Friends* (1978) and Jack Beatty's *The Rascal King* (1992). Surprised by the popularity of *The Last Hurrah*, Curley rode the wave by writing his own autobiography, *I'd Do It Again.*

Follow School Street down to the corner of Washington, where one of Boston's most curious structures — the building that once housed the **Old Corner Bookstore** — still stands. Built in 1718 as a home and

Old Corner Bookstore

apothecary shop by Dr. Thomas Crease, it served as home and office for a series of pharmacists and physicians for more than a hundred years. In the nineteenth century, however, it became an internationally known literary center — the simple site where **William D. Ticknor** (1810–1864) and **James T. Fields** (1817–1881) revolutionized American book publishing between 1845 and 1865.

Beginning in 1829, Carter & Hendee, then Ticknor & Allen, became the first of ten firms of booksellers and publishers to be based here over the next seventy-five years. By 1837, the young William Ticknor was running the show, assisted by a bright, witty, versatile, and ambitious apprentice named James T. Fields.

Before promoting Fields, then making him a partner, Ticknor ran a solid, nondescript shop that occasionally published books — usually at the authors' expense. Once Fields shared the helm, the Old Corner Bookstore was on the road to worldwide renown as a well-stocked shop, a prominent publishing house, and a magnet for the literary world.

To attract authors and secure exclusive publishing rights in the United States, Fields devised the first system of royalties. He also secured the ownership of prestigious magazines like the *North American Review* and the fledgling

James T. Fields, Nathaniel Hawthorne, and George Ticknor

will always mention the little Corner Bookstore in Boston . . . , and those who recall it in other days will always remember the curtained desk at which poet and philosopher and historian and divine, and the doubting, timid young author, were sure to see the bright face and to hear the hearty welcome of James T. Fields. What a crowded, busy shop it was, with the shelves full of books, and piles of books upon the counters and tables. . . . [Here, at the Old Corner Bookstore, was] the Exchange of Wit, the Rialto of current good things, the hub of the Hub. . . . It was a very remarkable group of men — indeed, it was the first group of really great American authors — which familiarly frequented the corner as guests of [James T.] Fields. . . . It was that circle which compelled the world to acknowledge that there was an American literature. Of most of these authors the house at the corner came to be the publishers, and to the end they maintained the warmest relations with Fields, who was not their publisher only, but their appreciative and sympathetic friend.

Atlantic Monthly, in which his writers regularly appeared.

A sincere friend, guardian, and literary counselor to his flock of writers, Fields was also an entrepreneurial huckster with a flair for promotion. He organized and publicized speaking tours — including Dickens's lucrative lecture circuit of 1867–1868 — and was not above "buying" reviewers, inventing facts about his authors, planting publicity in periodicals, and writing glowing reviews of his own books under fabricated names.

In *From the Easy Chair* (1892–1894), George William Curtis beautifully described the allure of Fields and the Old Corner: *The annals of publishing and the traditions of publishers in this country*

Among the dozens of prominent writers who worked with Ticknor & Fields — and who passed through the store's portals with startling regularity — were Harriet Beecher Stowe and Henry David Thoreau as well as Emerson, Longfellow, Holmes, Whittier, and Dickens. If Boston was "the Hub of the Solar System," the Old Corner

Bookstore was surely "the Hub of the Hub," as acknowledged in this comment from *Harper's Magazine*: *The Old Corner is so popular a resort that all Boston, with little exaggeration, may be said to pass through it in a day.*

James T. Fields had a special talent for uncovering, encouraging, and publishing gems by Boston's writers. One of his favorite stories, as recounted in *Yesterdays with Authors* (1871), was pulling a particular manuscript from the reclusive Nathaniel Hawthorne. True or not — and there is a question about its authenticity — it's nevertheless a fine tale: *I was hurrying down the stairs when [Hawthorne] called after me from the chamber, asking me to stop a moment. Then*

I never can go into that famous Corner Bookstore and look over the new books in the row before me, as I enter the door, without seeing half a dozen which I want to read or at least know about. The titles of many of them interest me. I look into one or two, perhaps. I have sometimes picked up a line of a sentence, in those momentary glances through the uncut leaves of a new book, which I have never forgotten.

— Oliver Wendell Holmes

---

quickly stepping into the entry with a roll of manuscript in his hands, he said: "How in Heaven's name did you know this thing was there? As you have found me out, take what I have written, and tell me, after you get home and have time to read it, if it is good for anything. It is either very good or very bad, — I don't know which."... On my way up to Boston I read the germ of "The Scarlet Letter."...

Of course, Fields had his literary misses as well. When a young teacher named Louisa May Alcott brought him some recent work, he responded, "Stick to your teaching; you can't write." He then loaned the young Alcott forty dollars for classroom books and chairs, saying she could return the cash if and when she made her fortune.

Three years after the roaring success of *Little Women* (1868), Alcott sent Fields the cash, along with a brief, bemused note:

Dear Mr. Fields

Once upon a time you lent me forty dollars, kindly saying I might return them when I had made 'a pot of gold.'

As the miracle has been unexpectedly wrought I wish to fulfil my part of the bargain, & herewith repay my debt with many thanks.

Very truly yours
L. M. ALCOTT

The Houghton Mifflin Publishing Company, still in Boston, is a

Annie Adams Fields, watercolor on ivory by Lucia Fairchild Fuller, based on an 1855 daguerreotype

Ticknor & Fields and Saturday Club groups as well as **Sarah Orne Jewett** (1849–1909) — Annie's companion for many years in a "Boston marriage" — and their protégée, Willa Cather. Other literary women supported by Annie Fields included the poet Louise Imogen Guiney and Harriet Beecher Stowe.

Oliver Wendell Holmes, in a Christmas letter to Annie Fields in 1881, recalled the galaxy of talent that congregated in her home: *Under your roof I have met more visitors to be remembered than under any other. But for your hospitality I should never have had the privilege of personal acquaintance with famous writers and artists whom I can now recall as I saw them, talked with them, heard them in that pleasant library, that most lively and agreeable dining-room.*

The site of the Old Corner Bookstore, incidentally, has literary connections that predate Ticknor & Fields by two centuries. Four years after Boston was settled by the English in 1630, **Anne Hutchinson** and her husband built a home on this corner. Hutchinson was a popular midwife and brilliant thinker who challenged the male Puritan hierarchy on their strict and exclusive religious and social viewpoints. A variety of similarly rebellious women — including the Quaker **Mary Dyer** — met regularly for discussion groups and

direct descendant of Ticknor & Fields.

James T. Fields's first wife, Eliza Josephine Willard, died a few months after their marriage in 1850. Four years later, Fields married Eliza's 19-year-old cousin, Annie Adams.

In time, **Annie Adams Fields** (1834–1915) became a cultural icon herself, holding court at salons for her literary, theatrical, and artistic friends in her home at 148 (originally 37) Charles Street. Her guests included many of the prayer at Hutchinson's home, soon threatening the Puritan status quo and ultimately dooming Hutchinson to banishment. Colonial Boston was clearly not ready to embrace her quest for freedom of speech and thought.

Other prominent neighbors from this early colonial period were Governor John Winthrop, whose journals chronicled the early history of Boston, and the **Reverend Cotton Mather** (ca. 1663–1728), whose numerous sermons comprised an essential element in colonial literature.

The Reverend Mather was one of many literary Mathers in the New World, beginning with his grandfather Richard (1596–1669), a contributor to the 1640 *Bay Psalm Book.* Cotton Mather, a Harvard graduate, had more than 2,000 volumes in his library. He also wrote 444 books of his own, including *The Wonders of the Invisible World* and the 1,300-page *Magnalia Christi Americana,* about the Salem witch trials. The powerful, persuasive Mather was hated by many, including the twentieth-century poet Robert Lowell, who observed that "the

The Reverend Cotton Mather

Salem witch-hanger was a professional man of letters employed to moralize and subdue. . . ."

Though the Old Corner Bookstore is an important landmark today, this was not always the case. In 1903, forty years after the departure of Ticknor & Fields, the last of the series of booksellers left, and the building went through a number of incarnations, from haberdashery to photo supply store. By 1960, the nearly unrecognizable, deteriorated structure held a pizza parlor plastered with outdoor billboards. Moreover, developers interested in urban renewal were eyeing the site as a prime spot for a parking lot.

The threat of demolition inspired a group of Bostonians — including the Athenaeum's director, Walter Muir Whitehill, and John Codman, chairman of the Beacon Hill Architectural Commission — to organize the non-profit Historic Boston Incorporated. With encouragement from the City of Boston, private donations from around the country, and a bank loan (which the *Boston Globe* later helped them repay), Historic

Boston took title to the building at the end of 1960. For the next twenty-five years, the historic exterior was restored and the interior modernized for retail and office spaces. Since then, the building has been used as a bookstore, *Boston Globe* offices, and the headquarters for Historic Boston and the Freedom Trail Foundation.

Diagonally across from the Old Corner Bookstore, at 310 Washington Street, is the **Old South Meeting House**, a pivotal meeting place for patriots at the onset of the American Revolution. Now a beautifully renovated and active cultural center and museum, the Old South congregation included two

Old South Meeting House

eighteenth-century literary lights: Phillis Wheatley, America's first published black poet, and Benjamin Franklin, who was born a stone's throw away. Franklin wrote his first prose while working nearby, at his brother's print shop on Court Street.

In the 1870s, the Old South was threatened with demolition. The philanthropist Mary Hemenway led the effort to save it, engaging some of Boston's most eminent citizens — Julia Ward Howe, Ralph Waldo Emerson, Louisa May Alcott, James Russell Lowell, and Wendell Phillips — to do public readings here and to plea for the building's salvation. Walter Muir Whitehill, a twentieth-century historian, praised America's first successful urban historic preservation venture, noting that saving the Old South was "the first instance in Boston where respect for the historical and architectural heritage of the city triumphed over considerations of profit, expediency, laziness, and vulgar convenience."

If you are on foot, you can take a side trip here. With the Old South on your left and the Old Corner behind you, follow Washington Street to the busy shopping district called Downtown Crossing. Four blocks from School Street, at 13–15 West Street, is a plaque marking the site of the **Elizabeth Peabody Book Shop.**

Elizabeth Peabody

Elizabeth Palmer Peabody (1804–1894) was a transcendentalist who founded America's first kindergarten and became the first female publisher in Boston. The store she ran at the front of her home on West Street became a vibrant literary gathering place, in part because she stocked many foreign books and periodicals. In the parlor behind the bookshop, Elizabeth's sister Mary was married to the educator Horace Mann and her sister Sophia, to Nathaniel Hawthorne.

Mary Peabody was a writer herself, seeking to improve humanity with such volumes as *The Flower People* and *Christianity in the Kitchen: A Physiological Cookbook.* **Sophia Peabody** was a painter and recluse who fell in love with the equally reclusive and terribly handsome Hawthorne, creating what contemporary author Shaun O'Connell called "one of the few happy marriages in American literary history."

The *grande dame* **Elizabeth Peabody** was a veritable legend in her own time — a moral teacher, educational reformer, abolitionist, feminist, biographer, publisher, and patron of the arts, who lived to the age of ninety. She supported the literary world tirelessly, joining Bronson Alcott's radical Temple School in 1834, helping Nathaniel Hawthorne secure a job at the Custom House, publishing Thoreau's "Civil Disobedience," paying for the publication of the *Dial,* the transcendentalist periodical, and inspiring those around her to reason, write, and create.

Though he flatly denied it, Henry James clearly used Elizabeth Peabody as a model for Miss Birdseye in *The Bostonians* (1886). Early in that novel, the feminist Olive Chancellor describes Birdseye — an ardent transcendentalist and devotee of Emerson — to the handsome southern intruder, Basil Ransom:

"And who is Miss Birdseye?"
"She is one of our celebrities. She is the woman in the world, I suppose, who has laboured most for every wise reform. I think I ought to tell you," Miss Chancellor went on in

a moment, "she was one of the earliest, one of the most passionate, of the old Abolitionists."

She had thought, indeed, she ought to tell him that, and it threw her into a little tremor of excitement to do so. Yet, if she had been afraid he would show some irritation at this news, she was disappointed at the geniality with which he exclaimed:

"Why, poor old lady — she must be quite mature!"

The most important literary events at Elizabeth Peabody's bookstore, however, were undoubtedly the "Conversations" held between 1839 and 1844 by the brilliant and intense **Margaret Fuller** (1810–1850). For five years, Wednesday afternoons at 15 West Street were devoted to stimulating discussions on topics as diverse as art, education, ethics, health, mythology, heroes, and women's rights. The women — and later, the men as well — Fuller attracted to her "Conversations" were a *Who's Who* of progressive Boston in the 1840s. As Fuller later explained: *[M]en are called on from an early period to reproduce all that they learn. Their college exercises, their political duties, their professional studies . . . call on them to put to use what they have learned. But women learn without any attempt to reproduce. Their only reproduction is for purposes of display. It is to supply this defect that these conversations have been planned.*

One significant outgrowth of these meetings was Fuller's magnum opus, *Woman in the Nineteenth Century* (1845), a groundbreaking exploration of early feminism.

Born in Cambridgeport in 1810 and raised by a stern father who would have preferred a boy, Margaret Fuller was rewarded with a boy's education: she was reading Ovid, Virgil, and Horace by the age of eight and was immersed in classical literature throughout her teen years; she was also the first woman to be allowed to use the Harvard College Library. In time, Fuller became a respected critic and pioneering female reporter for the *New York Tribune*. Having the brilliant "mind of a man" — not to

Margaret Fuller

mention a large-boned body and mannerisms that many considered masculine — Fuller was an intimidating presence. Equally disconcerting was her unwillingness to hide these strengths, as evidenced in this comment from *Memoirs of Margaret Fuller Ossoli* (1852): *I now know all the people worth knowing in America, and I find no intellect comparable to my own.*

Many of America's most respected thinkers — such as Bronson Alcott and Ralph Waldo Emerson — were clearly taken with Fuller's personal magnetism and accepted her as an intellectual equal. Alcott hired her to teach languages at his progressive Temple School. As a member of Emerson's Hedges Club, Fuller helped the philosopher develop the concept of transcendentalism; as an editor of the *Dial,* she and Emerson sustained a national showcase for essays by the cream of the trascendentalist crop. Julia Ward Howe, in her 1883 biography of Fuller, noted the differences between these two brilliant colleagues and friends: *While Mr. Emerson never appeared to be modified by any change of circumstance, never melted nor took fire, but was always and everywhere himself, the soul of Margaret was subject to a glowing passion which raised the temperature of the social atmosphere around her.*

Fuller's promising future was cut short in 1850. Returning home from Italy — where she covered the Italian revolt and secretly married Marquis Angelo Ossoli — her ship ran aground off Fire Island. Fuller, Ossoli, and their infant son all drowned. A distraught Emerson sent Thoreau to survey the wreckage, but no remnants of Fuller or Ossoli were ever found.

Fuller's dynamic persona lived on in memory and literature. It's likely, for example, that she provided the inspiration for many literary characters, including Zenobia in Hawthorne's *The Blithedale Romance* (1852) and Miranda in James Russell Lowell's *A Fable for Critics* (1848).

Retrace your path along Washington Street. One block before School Street you'll see Bromfield Street on your left and Franklin Street on your right. The Studio Building, at the corner of Bromfield and Tremont, was originally the working space for many artists. Daniel Chester French, a sculptor linked to Boston's literary history who appears throughout the Literary Trail, once shared studio space here.

Three blocks down Franklin Street, at the corner of Federal, is the site of the Federal Street (also known as Boston) Theater. Opened in 1794 as Boston's first legitimate theater, the Federal offered several decades of performances until it closed in 1852.

Among the writers whose plays

were produced here was **Susanna Haswell Rowson** (1762–1824), an English educator, school administrator, actor, lecturer, playwright, poet, and novelist who made her home in Boston. Rowson is best known for her morality tale for young women, *Charlotte Temple* (1791), which remained America's best-selling novel until 1852, when Harriet Beecher Stowe's *Uncle Tom's Cabin* took its place.

Newspaper Row, 1889

A contemporary of Rowson's was **Judith Sargent Murray** (1751–1820), whose satirical works for the stage, *The Medium or Happy Tea Party* and *The Traveller Returned*, were produced at the Federal Street Theater in 1795 and 1796. Murray was well respected as a poet for a variety of Boston journals and a regular columnist for the *Massachusetts Magazine*, where, under a male pseudonym, she discussed women's equality, politics, and education. When these columns were collected in her book, *The Gleaner* (1798), Murray became the first American woman to publish her own work.

Return to the corner of Washing-

ton and School streets, by the new Irish Famine Memorial (1998). The literary tradition lives on in this historic area of Boston, with bookstores offering ample volumes on the city's social and political heritage. Not far from here are several other sites important in America's literary history.

From the nineteenth through the middle of the twentieth century, the area around Washington, Court, and State streets was known as **Newspaper Row**. This strip was once the home of many of Boston's most powerful newspapers — including the *Boston Globe*, the *Transcript*, the *Herald*, the *Post*, the *Traveller*, and the *Journal* — and was renowned as "the Cradle of American Journalism." Off Washington Street is the long alcove known as **Pi Alley**, so named for the small jumbles of press type often strewn about here.

Though Bostonians today have grown used to seeing two daily newspapers, the *Boston Globe* and the *Boston Herald*, their forebears were offered many more newspapers, and many more editions. In *The Proper Bostonians* (1947), Cleveland Amory mused on the heyday of the old *Transcript*, the Hub's society rag, whose offices stood at the corner of Milk and Washington streets: *It is doubtful if Boston's institution men would ever have achieved such prominence in their city if they had not had a voice to carry their "way of life" to the Proper Bostonian masses. They found this voice in one of the all-time curiosities of American journalism, the Boston* Evening Transcript. . . . *Not to read the* Transcript *was unthinkable. It was never a newspaper in the vulgar sense of the word. The story of three representatives of the press who were received into a Beacon Hill home with a servant's announcement, "Two reporters from the papers, Sir, and a gentleman from the* Transcript," *was actually a legend once removed from the London* Times, *but it became the Boston paper's trademark. The loyalty of its readers was proverbial. In the wind of its editorial opinion they swayed, said the poet T.S. Eliot, "like a field of ripe corn."*

This section of Washington Street, Boston's oldest thoroughfare, was originally called Cornhill. Even in colonial and early federal times, it was a bustling center of book publishing and sales. Edgar Allan Poe's first book, *Tamerlane and Other Poems*, was published anonymously in 1827 in a building at the corner of Washington and State (formerly King) streets.

At the corner of King and Kirby streets was the home of the successful tailor and merchant John Wheatley and his wife, Susanna. When a frail, sickly child of seven or eight arrived in Boston in 1761 on a slave ship from West Africa, she was purchased by the Wheatleys to be a household servant. They called the girl "Phillis" after the slave ship and "Wheatley" after her owners.

Postcard of Pi Alley, circa 1910

Patricia Smith on Phillis Wheatley

A blade edge glints from the vowels
of such simple words, written in
nervous, new girl cursive — there were
never chains to escape from, only
her own skin, black prison, sweet cage.
She endured the pale, well-meaning hands
patting her head, resting on the tamed naps
of her hair, she smiled while men cooed
in awed praise of those slices from her soul,
those rhythm shrieks, those prayers out loud
set down in neat couplets, line after chopped line
of words she wasn't supposed to know.
Such a good girl, so smart, well-spoken,
crisp blouse buttoned tight at her throat,
writing words right enough to sing, almost
like she was
free.

She wrote of freedom so deftly, there seemed
to be no reason she couldn't rise from her desk
and walk into the shelter of a million waiting arms,
no reason she couldn't open her mouth wide,
throw back her head, pop loose imprisoned hips
and dance until the pink bottoms of her feet
were threaded with soul. There were never
real chains to escape from, only this dream
she kept having, the feel of a million white hands
resting proudly on her head. Each time she
wrote of freedom, tasted its potent mix
of iron and sunlight, she remembered Boston.

America's first face, breathing outside her window.
Boston was a skewered rhyme, books with
gilt-edged pages, the flat smack of a whip
on the flanks of a tired horse. Boston was
her teacher, her captor, her crotchety muse,
taunting her with the promise of free,
a wild someday dance on weary feet.
She was lucky. Boston was the perfect place
to settle behind a desk of scarred wood,
light a candle, dip an old pen into pitch-black ink,
touch that pen to paper, and begin to scream again.

Under the tutelage of Susanna and her teenage twins, Nathaniel and Mary, **Phillis Wheatley** (ca. 1753–1784) learned to speak, read, and write English in only sixteen months. She also studied Latin, geography, history, the classics, and the Bible, and she was writing poetry by the age of twelve. Her first poem was "On the Reverend Joseph Sewall When Sick," about the pastor of the Old South Meeting House, whose congregation she joined in 1771.

Phillis Wheatley

Poetry eventually brought Phillis international fame. When her first book — *Poems on Various Subjects, Religious and Moral* (1773) — was rejected by a Boston printer, she published it with the bookseller and publisher Archibald Bell in London, supported by Selina Hastings, the countess of Huntington. And when some expressed doubt that a slave could have written such excellent verse, Phillis submitted to an interrogation by a panel of men — including seven ministers, Governor Thomas Hutchinson, and John Hancock — and passed with the highest praise.

Though many have criticized the quality of Wheatley's verse, her style reflected the popular tastes of the day and included many elegies and tributes to God or great men, with themes of learning, virtue, and redemption through Christ. One such poem, dedicated to General George Washington of the Continental Army, earned her warm thanks and an invitation to Washington's headquarters in Cambridge. That house is now known for a later owner who lived there for many years, Henry Wadsworth Longfellow.

Proceed, great chief, with virtue on thy side,
Thy every action let the goddess guide.
A crown, a mansion, and a throne that shine,
With gold unfading, WASHINGTON! be thine.
— Phillis Wheatley, "To His Excellency George Washington" (1775)

Benjamin Franklin

ist William Lloyd Garrison hid in 1835, when an angry mob tried to lynch him for his views. The Bostonian Society, which operates a stellar library of Boston history across the way, has run the Old State House as a museum since 1882.

To reach Faneuil Hall, take a right turn down State Street past the Old State House, then a left on Congress Street.

Faneuil Hall, opened in 1742 and enlarged by Charles Bulfinch in 1805, was called "the Cradle of Liberty" — a term later applied to all of Boston. From its stage Samuel Adams advocated the overthrow of British rule, William Lloyd Garrison appealed for an end to slavery, Susan B. Anthony denounced the inferior status of women, and John F. Kennedy gave his final speech before winning the presidency in 1960.

The ground-level shops under Faneuil Hall and the numerous Faneuil Hall Marketplace stores nearby are a shopper's and food lover's paradise, with several well-stocked bookstores to boot.

At the intersection of Washington, State, and Court streets, you are facing the Old State House and the downtown Visitor Center for the Boston National Historical Park.

Though not a part of the Literary Trail, the Old State House and Faneuil Hall — two blocks farther down Congress Street — are both significant stops on the Revolutionary Freedom Trail and landmarks of free speech in America.

At the Old State House, the colonial patriot and lawyer James Otis argued against the Writs of Assistance, paving the way for the American Revolution. Here the Declaration of Independence was first read aloud to the town of Boston in 1776, and here abolition-

Return to the Old State House, at the junction of Court and Washington streets. As you go up Court Street, you'll pass on the right a plaque marking the site of the *New-England Courant*, one of Boston's earliest newspapers. When James Franklin began the *Courant* in 1721, he created the fourth newspaper ever printed in the British colonies. More important, he quickly attracted some of the quickest, cleverest, and most rebellious writers around — including his younger brother Ben.

Benjamin Franklin (1706–1790), the fifteenth of seventeen Franklin children, was not hired as a writer. At the age of twelve, Ben began an arduous, often cruel and exploitative nine-year apprenticeship to James. Despite only two years of formal education, Ben was bright, well read, and self-confident. Between his menial duties at the newspaper, he read from James's ample library, absorbed the insights of the *Courant*'s writers, learned Boston inside and out, and mastered the skills of editing, printing, and distributing a newspaper.

Unbeknownst to his brother, Ben also became a popular columnist. For six months in 1722, Ben secretly composed and submitted to the paper a series of fourteen

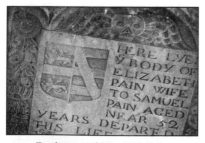

Tombstone of Elizabeth Pain,
King's Chapel Burying Ground

witty, often wise and biting essays on topics from virginity, hoop petticoats, and insincere funeral elegies to the quality of education at Harvard and the cultural life of the Commonwealth. Under the whimsical moniker of Silence Dogood — an imaginary widow of a Harvard minister — Ben also touched on women's liberation and the poverty of widowhood. Slipped under James's door at night, the columns had an impact on Boston's social and political life — not to mention its gossip.

The ruse didn't last. Nor did Ben's willingness to complete his apprenticeship in the repressive Puritan town of Boston. At seventeen, he moved to New York, then Philadelphia, and became the philosopher, essayist, newspaperman, diplomat, politician, scientist, and inventor we recall today.

Follow Court up to Tremont Street, bearing left on Tremont to the **King's Chapel Burying Ground**. Boston's oldest graveyard was visited by Nathaniel Hawthorne when he worked at the Custom House or did research at the Boston Athenaeum. James T. Fields, in *Yesterdays with Authors* (1871), recalled Hawthorne's affinity for burying grounds: *He very rarely described himself as* inside *a church, but he liked to wander among the graves in the churchyards and read the epitaphs on the moss-grown slabs.*

Since the 1920s, the legend has grown that the gravestone of Elizabeth Pain (d. 1704) inspired the character of Hester Prynne in Hawthorne's great novel *The Scarlet Letter* (1850). Though the connection has never been substantiated and is unlikely, the heraldic symbol on Pain's grave, on the path nearest the side wall of King's Chapel, can be vaguely seen to resemble a stylized "A." Inspired by Pain's headstone or not, the vision of Hester Prynne's grave provided Hawthorne with a chilling finish to his novel:

And, after many, many years, a new grave was delved, near an old and sunken one, in that burial-ground beside which King's Chapel has since been built. . . . All around there were monuments carved with armorial bearings; and on this simple slab of slate . . . there appeared the semblance of an engraved escutcheon . . . "ON A FIELD, SABLE, THE LETTER A, GULES."

Continue down Tremont Street, past the Omni Parker House on your left. Stop for a moment by **Tremont Temple**, an active Baptist church whose roots go back to the early nineteenth century. The original structure was the old Tremont Theater, which opened in 1827. By 1840, however, Boston's theaters were beseiged by religious revivalists who considered public stages bastions of immorality. Hence, in 1843, the structure was sold to a new Baptist congregation, which espoused the radical concept that blacks and whites could worship together in complete equality. What was called the First Baptist Free Church became the first truly integrated church in America.

Though the building (in four different incarnations) has been a house of worship ever since, it never abandoned the theatrical world. Even during its first decade, Tremont Temple was continually leased to producers of plays and musical events as well as to political orators and writers.

Abraham Lincoln spoke here, as did every American president thereafter through Herbert Hoover. Daniel Webster waxed eloquent, as did Edward Everett, William Lloyd Garrison, Frederick Douglass, Eugene Debs, Helen Keller, the Reverend Billy Sunday, the Reverend Billy Graham, and a host of others. Sitting in the audience, Harriet Beecher Stowe was given a standing ovation when the Emancipation Proclamation was first read aloud here in 1863. And when Charles Dickens gave theatrical readings during his 1867–1868 American tour, he packed the house at Tremont Temple every night.

During one of Will Rogers's visits to Boston in 1930, he attended a service at Tremont Temple Baptist Church. Asked by the press to say a few words, Rogers quipped, "When

I die, my epitaph . . . is going to read, 'I joked about every prominent man of my time, but I never met a man I didn't like.' I am proud of that. I can hardly wait to die so it can be carved."

The remark was connected to the humorist forever after.

Farther down Tremont is the **Granary Burying Ground**, the permanent home of many heroes of the American Revolution: the firebrand Samuel Adams, the revolutionary bankroller John Hancock, the impassioned orator James Otis, the five victims of the Boston Massacre, and the midnight rider, Paul Revere. The family of Benjamin Franklin is also buried here.

The Granary's most curious link to Boston literary history, however, is the alleged gravesite of "Mother Goose." Boston's Mother Goose was **Elizabeth Foster** (1665–1757), the second wife of Isaac Goose or "Vergoose," or perhaps even "Vertigoose." According to one version of the tale, Elizabeth fed, raised, and told stories to sixteen Goose children — six of her own and ten by Isaac's first wife. Another version suggests that she told her grand-

children these stories during her years as a widow. These tales were supposedly collected and published in 1719 by her son-in-law Thomas Fleet as *Songs for the Nursery or Mother Goose's Melodies for Children.*

Though the legend endures, it's not likely that Mother Goose is spending eternity at the Granary. One problem is, she has no headstone. Isaac is here, as is his first wife, Mary. But no marker suggests that Elizabeth is by their side. Second, there is no copy extant of Fleet's volume. Moreover, both France and England claim to have nurtured the *real* Mother Goose — and most of the rhymes we know today can be traced to European origins.

Sarah Josepha Buell Hale

One of America's most popular nursery rhymes did, however, originate with a Boston woman. A patriotic widow named **Sarah Josepha Buell Hale** (1788–1879) organized a glorified bake sale in 1830 to finance the completion of the Bunker Hill Monument; she also helped to convince Abraham Lincoln to declare Thanksgiving a national holiday in 1863.

Though she wrote poems, short

stories, plays, novels, and a women's encyclopedia, Hale is best known as one of America's first female editors. She edited and published the *Ladies Magazine* (1828–1837) in Boston before moving to Philadelphia to run the popular *Godey's Lady's Book* (1837–1877). Though the latter often featured mediocre writing and sentimental fluff, it also included contributions from Emerson, Longfellow, Stowe, Poe, and Hawthorne.

Hale's most enduring work was a famous nursery rhyme, first published in *Poems for Our Children* (1830) as "Mary's Lamb":

Mary had a little lamb,
Its fleece was white as snow,
And everywhere that Mary went,
That lamb was sure to go.

Just beyond the Granary, at the corner of Tremont and Park streets, is the **Park Street Church**, which Henry James once called "the most interesting mass of bricks and mortar" in the country. Two important events occurred here on the Fourth of July. In 1829, William Lloyd Garrison gave his first public antislavery address, and in 1831, the song "America" was first sung from the steps of the church. Popularly known as "My Country 'Tis of Thee," the lyrics were written by Samuel Francis Smith of Boston, who was then preparing for the ministry at Andover Theological Seminary.

Across the street is the **Park Street Station** of the Massachusetts Bay Transportation Authority (MBTA). Opened in 1897, this was one of the four original stops on America's first subway system. This beloved old station and its subway have been heralded in sonnet and song over the past century: Oliver Wendell Holmes waxed poetic about it in "The Broomstick Train," A. J. Deutsch wrote an eerie science fiction tale about a train bound for Cambridge in "A Subway Named Mobius" (1950), and the Kingston Trio had a smash hit in 1959 with their song about poor Charlie, who failed to pay the five-cent fare hike:

Charlie's wife goes down to the
*   Scollay Square Station*
Every day at quarter past two,
And through the open window she
*   hands Charlie a sandwich*
As the train comes rumblin'
*   through.*

Did he ever return? He never
*   returned,*
And his fate is still unlearned.
He may ride forever through the
*   streets of Boston,*
He's the man who never returned.

Incidentally, "M.T.A." was originally composed in 1949 by Bess Lomax Hawes and Jacqueline Steiner as a campaign ditty for the Progressive Party's candidate for mayor of Boston, Walter O'Brien. (O'Brien lost to John Hynes.)

Turn right up Park Street, toward the State House.

In recent decades the building on the corner of Park and Beacon has housed various dining, café, and retail spaces. More than a century ago, however, the old **Amory-Ticknor House** was where the educator George Ticknor (1791–1871) wrote his best-known work, *History of Spanish Literature*, over a period of two decades.

A cousin of William Ticknor's, of the Old Corner Bookstore, George began the first courses in Spanish and French literature and language at Harvard to supplement the traditional Greek and Latin. Among his best students were Henry David Thoreau, James Russell Lowell, John Lothrop Motley, Francis James Child, and Charles Eliot Norton. When Ticknor resigned from Harvard in 1835, his friend Henry Wadsworth Longfellow took his place.

Ticknor also helped found the Boston Public Library, giving it his own extensive collection — some 18,000 volumes. He traveled throughout Europe, meeting the great writers of the day, including Lord Byron and Madame de Staël. These travels not only helped inspire his students but also enabled him to purchase books for the Boston library.

If you're on foot, a brief side trip will prove worthwhile. As you face

The Boston Athenaeum

the gold dome of the State House, bear right onto Beacon to visit the **Boston Athenaeum**, discreetly set back at 10½. In 1851, with a collection of some 50,000 volumes, it was one of the five largest libraries in the nation. (Its main competitor was the Library of Congress.)

Incorporated in 1807 as a private reading room, library, and art museum, the Boston Athenaeum became a haven for artists, writers, and their well-bred Brahmin backers. The oldest cultural institution and largest membership library in North America, the Athenaeum also helped establish Boston's Museum of Fine Arts in 1876, providing much of the museum's early artwork. The current building, designed by Edward Clarke Cabot, was opened in 1849.

One of the finest descriptions of the Athenaeum was written by the poet, essayist, and anthologist **David McCord** (1897–1997) in his gentle and witty book, *About Boston* (1948): *Number 10½ Beacon Street, overlooking The Granary Burying Ground — as every literate American knows — is the address of the Boston Athenaeum. Though not the oldest of stockholders' libraries in America, it is easily the most famous and prosperous of them all. . . . From 1822 to 1849 you would have found it down on Pearl Street. But it is in the present original and otherworldly building that the Athenaeum has grown in tradition and influence. No other Boston institution has anything like its unique, endearing, and enduring atmosphere. It combines the best elements of the Bodleian, Monticello, the frigate* Constitution, *a greenhouse, and an old New England sitting room. . . . The Athenaeum is a kind of Utopia for books: the high-ceilinged rooms, the little balconies, alcoves, nooks and angles all suggest sanctuary, escape, creature comfort. The reader, the scholar, the browser, the borrower is king.*

A repository for many important original works — from paintings and statuary to the book collections of George Washington and Henry Knox — the Boston Athenaeum has served prestigious scholars for almost two centuries. Typical among its nineteenth-century members was Ralph Waldo Emerson, who would take the train from his home in Concord, then visit the Old Corner Bookstore and the Athenaeum before dining at the Parker House. Less typical, perhaps, was Nathaniel Hawthorne, who communed with the polite ghost of one Reverend Thaddeus Mason Harris in the Pearl Street Athenaeum's reading room in 1842, while the specter was browsing over the *Boston Post.*

Harris was an industrious, wise, and withered man, whose lifetime had been spent ministering to his Unitarian flock in Dorchester, as well as joining the active ranks of groups like the Massachusetts Historical Society, the Humane Society, the Massachusetts Horticultural Society, and the Boston Athenaeum. On the day of Harris's death, however, Nathaniel Hawthorne began running into the late reverend's unsuspecting specter, couched in his customary chair near the fireplace in the Athe-

> [The Athenaeum] was to Boston as large as Boston at large was to the rest of New England.
>
> — Henry James, *The American Scene* (1907)

naeum's reading room. As he described it later, Hawthorne was baffled about what to do: *After a certain period — I really know not how long — I began to notice . . . a peculiar regard in the old gentleman's aspect towards myself. I sometimes found him gazing at me, and, unless I deceived myself, there was some sort of expectancy in his face. . . . Being a ghost, and amenable to ghostly laws, it was natural that he was waiting to be spoken to before delivering whatever message he had to impart. . . . In the reading room of the Athenaeum conversation is strictly forbidden, and I could not have addressed the apparition without drawing the instant notice and indignant frowns of the slumberous old gentlemen around me. I myself, too, at that time, was as shy as any ghost, and followed the ghost's rule never to speak first.*

Though long considered a bastion of conservatism, the Athenaeum has also been a gathering place for more than its share of nineteenth-century radicals and twentieth-century progressives.

In the 1820s, when women were often excluded from colleges and libraries, **Hannah Adams** (1755–1831), a distant relative of the statesman John Adams, was allowed to study here and was even granted full access by 1827. However, the woman heralded as America's first full-time professional female author was locked inside the library during the lunch hour so she could pursue her studies "in modesty." Adams's popular works include *A Summary History of New England* (1799), *The Truth and Excellence of the Christian Religion Exhibited* (1804), and *The History of the Jews* (1812).

When **Lydia Maria Child** (1802–1880) wrote an immediatist antislavery tract, *An Appeal in Favor of that Class of Americans Called Africans* (1833), she found her Athenaeum privileges mysteriously revoked. And when that pamphlet was exhibited at Ticknor's Old Corner Bookstore, an irate crowd smashed the shop's windows. Boston society in the 1830s was not ready to embrace abolitionism — especially those who favored the *immediate* aboli-

Lydia Maria Child

Amy Lowell

*Over the river and through the
 wood,
To grandfather's house we go;
The horse knows the way
To carry the sleigh
Through the white and drifted snow.*

Another less than traditional early member was the cigar-smoking **Amy Lowell** (1874–1925) — who ordered 10,000 Manila cigars in 1915, anticipating a wartime shortage. Born in Brookline, Massachusetts, to the famed New England Lowells, Amy grew from an inveterate tomboy into a radical poet and popular celebrity. Given free rein of the Athenaeum from childhood, Lowell was in literary heaven. In 1912 and 1913, her discovery of the actress Ada Dwyer Russell, the revolutionary *Poetry* magazine, and a subsequent trip to Europe — where she encountered Ezra Pound and the new school of "imagist" poetry — solidified her commitment to verse. Over the next dozen years, she edited or wrote ten books of verse as well as a biography of John Keats. Sought after as a

tion of slavery — though its landscape would change dramatically in the next three decades.

Child was known by her contemporaries as a writer of abolitionist literature, romantic novels, household guides, and didactic fiction. Her best-selling romance novel, *Hobomok* (1824), for example, had an underlying theme of racial tolerance, while her popular book *The Frugal Housewife* (1829) guided married women to better household management.

Today, Lydia Maria Child is remembered for less political work, notably her Thanksgiving verse from *Flowers for Children* (1844–1846):

Heart-leaves of lilac all over
 New England,
Roots of lilac under all the soil
 of New England,
Lilac in me because I am New
 England.

— Amy Lowell, *Lilacs*

speaker on both sides of the Atlantic, Lowell was also the first woman appointed to a position of authority at the Athenaeum. Her collection *What's O'Clock?* was awarded a Pulitzer Prize posthumously in 1926.

Augustus Saint-Gaudens, Robert Gould Shaw/54th Regiment Memorial

The writers who currently frequent the Athenaeum are equally well known. They include Doris Kearns Goodwin (*The Fitzgeralds and the Kennedys*), David McCullough (*Truman*), and the filmmaker Ken Burns (*The Civil War*).

Walter Muir Whitehill (1905–1978) was the director and librarian of the Athenaeum from 1946 to 1973. A concerned citizen and chronicler of Hub history — who helped to save the Old Corner Bookstore building from demolition in 1960 — Whitehill wrote several accessible and well-researched books, including the centennial histories *The Boston Public Library* (1956) and *The Museum of Fine Arts* (1970). His 1959 study, *Boston: A Topographical History,* remains the classic of its genre.

The Athenaeum's home on Beacon Street is closed for major renovation until sometime in 2001.

Directly across from the Athenaeum, 21 Beacon is now a building of condominiums, with restaurants and convenience stores at street level. It was once the ornate and lovely **Bellevue Hotel**, where Louisa May Alcott periodically rented rooms during several cold winters between 1874 and 1878. Sometimes she shared the Bellevue's "sky parlor" with other women reformers or let her younger sister May teach drawing in her apartments. The maternal grandparents of John F. Kennedy also rented an apartment suite here for a dozen years during the World War II era. Fifteen years before his election to the presidency, JFK occasionally stayed here when visiting family and running for Congress.

Kennedy's statue is a block away, in front of the State House.

Continuing up Beacon Street toward the crest of old Beacon Hill, notice the large high-relief sculpture across from the State House. The **Robert Gould Shaw /54th**

Regiment Memorial honors Colonel Shaw and his African-American volunteer regiment, who lost their lives during the Civil War — a tale beautifully retold in the 1989 film *Glory*.

The famed 54th, the first free black regiment of the Union Army, was formed shortly after President Lincoln issued the Emancipation Proclamation in January 1863. The troop's commanders were all white men, led by Colonel Robert Gould Shaw, a twenty-five-year-old Harvard dropout and the son of a prominent abolitionist family, who had already seen action at Antietam and Cedar Mountain.

Still, Shaw's African-American soldiers — recruited and trained at

John Greenleaf Whittier

Camp Meigs in Readville, near the modern neighborhood of Hyde Park — were, in the words of Governor John Andrew, "full of hope and glory." The 54th was the regiment many hoped would dispel American racism by proving that black soldiers were as skilled and brave as white soldiers. It was this regiment that would fight for pay equal to that of the white troops and for the opportunity to rise within the ranks and become officers.

By the time Shaw and his finely tuned regiment of 1,000 marched through the streets of Boston on May 28, 1863, Shaw had already observed, "There is not the least doubt that we shall leave the State with as good a regiment as any that has marched." Throngs came out to cheer as the 54th filed past the State House, then marched down toward Battery Wharf, where the steamer *De Molay* waited to take them to battlefields in the South

Many of New England's most progressive thinkers, writers, and abolitionists came together for this day of unity and community in Boston. Even the pacifist poet John Greenleaf Whittier attended, as he later wrote to Lydia Maria Child: *The only regiment I ever looked upon during the war was the 54th Massachusetts on its departure for the South. I can never forget the scene as Colonel Shaw rode at the head of his men. The very flower of*

**Boston Common and the
Massachusetts State House**

Lincoln Kirstein, and many others. One of the most memorable and moving pieces about the memorial — from the tumultuous civil rights period of the 1960s — was Robert Lowell's "For the Union Dead" (1964):

*Two months after marching through
    Boston,
half the regiment was dead;
at the dedication,
William James could almost hear the
    bronze
Negroes breathe.*

*Their monument sticks like a
    fishbone
in the city's throat.
Its Colonel is as lean
as a compass-needle.*

*He has an angry wrenlike vigilance,
a greyhound's gentle tautness;
he seems to wince at pleasure,
and suffocate for privacy.*

grace and chivalry, he seemed to me beautiful and awful, as an angel of God come down to lead the host of freedom to victory.

Thirty-four years after the 54th's gallant rush on Fort Wagner, South Carolina — in which the colonel and many of his troops were brutally slaughtered — Boston paid tribute with this grand memorial. Among those who spoke at its 1897 dedication were Booker T. Washington, the founder and president of Tuskegee Institute in Alabama, and the philosopher William James, whose brothers, Robertson and Garth Wilkinson James, had served as officers under Shaw.

Sculpted by the eminent Augustus Saint-Gaudens, Boston's finest piece of public art has inspired prose and poetry from the pens of James Russell Lowell, Ralph Waldo Emerson, Charles Ives, Luis Emilio,

Though the **Massachusetts State House** is more closely associated with politics than pens, one particular event provoked an assemblage of literary greats on the steps below. The planned execution of the Italian immigrants Nicola Sacco and Bartolomeo Vanzetti in 1927 aroused worldwide demonstrations of sympathy. Among those who adamantly protested the conduct of the trial and, ultimately, the electrocution were the prominent writers Edna St. Vincent Millay, John Dos Passos, and Upton Sinclair.

Sinclair's 1928 novel, entitled simply *Boston*, was based on the Sacco-Vanzetti trial — and banned in Boston by the ever-vigilant New England Watch and Ward Society. In intimate and intricate detail, Sinclair spun the tale of the two anarchists, whom he viewed as innocent victims of America's post-war xenophobia, the Red Scare of the 1920s, and a patently unfair legal process: *All day long the pickets would come, one batch after another, ten or twenty at a time, with their placards of polite protest, all bad words barred. They would walk their appointed number of paces, and then the police would close about them, and take them in tow, and march them . . . to the police-station. . . . There were well-known names among them. Edna St. Vincent Millay, from Rockland, Maine, home of her ancestors for many generations. Loveliest of woman poets, she would find this a devastating experience; life would not seem the same after a rendezvous with murder.*

Into the darkness they go, the wise and the lovely. Crowned With lilies and with laurel they go; but I am not resigned.

— Edna St. Vincent Millay,
Dirge Without Music
(1928)

Among those whose statues stand in front of the State House are two free-thinking colonial women, Anne Hutchinson and Mary Dyer. Hutchinson was banished from Boston for her heretical views on religious freedom; Dyer, a practicing Quaker, was hanged by the Puritans for largely similar reasons.

For many years, the sculptures of Hutchinson and Dyer were the only two pieces of outdoor art in the city that depicted actual women (though idealized female forms representing Freedom, Faith, Knowledge, Art, Grief, and the like have long been favorite motifs). In the late 1990s, however, steps were taken to rectify this situation. A new memorial representing three Boston women has been commissioned for the Commonwealth Avenue Mall. Meanwhile, a project initiated by the Massachusetts legislature has helped fund "Hear Us," a public art installation by Sheila Levrant de Bretteville and Susan Sellers commemorating the contributions of women to public life and social justice in Massachusetts. A mixed-media portrait gallery featuring six women from Boston now lines the walls inside the left front entrance to the State House. Two of the women are known for their literary contributions, Lucy Stone and Josephine St. Pierre Ruffin.

An abolitionist, feminist, and popular speaker, **Lucy Stone**

(1818–1893) was the first woman in Massachusetts to earn a college degree. When she married the reformer Henry Brown Blackwell, she kept her maiden name. This radical act inspired other women to follow her lead, earning them the nickname "Lucy Stoners." Stone founded and funded the Boston *Women's Journal* in 1870, which became a weekly newspaper and major voice of the American Woman Suffrage Association.

Lucy Stone

Even in death, Stone was unusually modern for her time. She was cremated at the facility that is now part of Forest Hills Cemetery — one of New England's first cremations, performed in Boston's first, and only, crematory.

Josephine St. Pierre Ruffin (1842–1924), who lived on Charles Street, was the African-American publisher and editor of *The Women's Era*, the first newspaper in America created by and for black women. A socially and politically active link between the city's wealthy white reformers and its African-American elite, Ruffin was the first person to join the New England Women's Club, whose founders included Julia Ward Howe and Lucy Stone. A member of the New England Women's Press Association, Ruffin helped to establish the New Era Club for African-American Women and cofounded the National Federation of Afro-American Women, a precursor of the National Association of Colored Women.

Though today associated with landscaped paths, public monuments, ranger-led walks, concerts, festivals, ball games, street vendors, protests, a skating pond, an underground parking garage, and stops for subways and tourist trolleys, **Boston Common** — on the slopes below the State House — was once used for more unusual pastimes.

That forty-eight-acre stretch of common land, set aside by the town for shared use in 1634, was the first public green in America. It was thus a perfect site for Mary Dyer's hanging, which took place from the Great Elm that once stood here. The young Ralph Waldo Emerson was said to have grazed his mother's cows on the Common

— a practice continued until 1830. Meanwhile, the relatively open Common served as a military training field, public burying ground, preacher's pulpit, scene of public punishment, deer park, and balloon launching pad, among other pursuits.

David McCord summed up the Common's broad appeal in *About Boston* (1948): *Boston Common is an ancient battleground of ideas and beliefs and freedoms — unmarked by pyramids of cannon balls, unrelieved by crosses to the fallen, as void of redoubt as of the mischievous doubt in the worst ancestral skull. . . . The hanging of four Quakers simply for being Quakers is perhaps the darkest chapter. . . . It is impossible even to attempt a three-hundred-year summary of the uses to which the Common at large has been put. Emerson as a boy drove a cow to pasture there; and cows were not put on the Common black list until 1830. [Military drills], fireworks, kite flying, snipe shooting, carpet beating, Punch and Judy shows, telescopes, coasting, the long coast on what were called monster double rippers . . . Whig mass meetings, anti-slavery meetings, a railroad jubilee, promenade concerts, conventions, Indian dances, sermons, the secluded smokers' circle, three hundred spinsters spinning . . . the Common has seen, known, heard or been them all.*

It's likely that every great literary figure who lived in or visited Boston once walked across the rolling acreage of the Common. The most famous pair to ramble here, however, may well have been **Walt Whitman** (1819–1892) and the adult Emerson.

Whitman espoused a literary eroticism — and, on occasion, homoeroticism — that gnawed at Victorian morals. Emerson invited Whitman on a lengthy walk across the Common in 1860 and tried to convince him to delete some of the racier passages from his 1855 opus, *Leaves of Grass*. Whitman did not waver, and the work was periodically banned throughout the country over the ensuing decades.

"Each point of Emerson's statement was unanswerable," observed Whitman, "no judge's charge ever

Walt Whitman

more complete or convincing. I could never hear the point better put — and then I felt down in my soul the clear and unmistakable conviction to disobey all, and pursue my own way." Meanwhile, Emerson registered his esteemed colleague as a guest at the Boston Athenaeum.

Another nineteenth-century writer — the irrepressible **Oliver Wendell Holmes, Sr.** (1809–1894) — immortalized one particular walkway on the Common. The so-called Long Path runs from the Guild Steps, where Joy Street meets Beacon, to the corner of Tremont and Boylston. Here, in his *Autocrat of the Breakfast Table* (1865), Holmes meandered with a certain schoolmistress: *At last I got out the question, — Will you take the long path with me? — Certainly, — said the schoolmistress, — with much pleasure. — Think, — I said, — before you answer: if you take the long path with me now, I shall interpret it that we are to part no more, and so it was.*

Though educated in law and medicine — he was Harvard's first Parkman Professor of Anatomy

and Physiology, dean of Harvard Medical School, and a founder of the American Medical Association — Oliver Wendell Holmes was the man who made Boston "the Hub of the Solar System." He first used that phrase in his popular and amusing columns called "Autocrat of the Breakfast Table," most of which ran in the *Atlantic Monthly* and were later collected in book form. (His words were later misquoted and remembered as "Hub of the Universe.")

Holmes's first literary piece was his poem "Old Ironsides" (1830), which inspired Bostonians to save the historic USS *Constitution* from demolition. Though he published important medical works, it was his witty, urbane, poetic, and sometimes sentimental writing and public speaking that caught the public's attention. Holmes was not only a major contributor to the *Atlantic Monthly,* he was also the man who named it. When James Russell Lowell became its first editor in 1857, it was with the tacit understanding that Holmes would be a regular contributor.

Oliver Wendell Holmes, Sr.

In more recent years, Boston Common has been a pulpit for international personalities such as Pope John Paul II and the **Reverend Martin Luther King, Jr.** (1929–1968), who called for racial equality in a grand civil rights rally.

On April 23, 1965, some 50,000 people marched three miles, from Roxbury to the Common, to protest racial discrimination in the northern as well as southern states. In his speech to this gathering, King declared: *I come not to condemn but to encourage. I would be dishonest to say Boston is Birmingham or that Massachusetts is a Mississippi. But it would be irresponsible for me to deny the crippling poverty and the injustices that exist in some sections of this community.*

The grandson of a slave, King was a Baptist clergyman and lead-

> I have a dream that my four little children will one day live in a nation where they will not be judged by the color of their skin but by the content of their character.
>
> I have a dream today.
>
> — Martin Luther King, Jr., Civil Rights March on Washington, 1963

ing civil rights activist committed to the style of nonviolent protest advocated by Mahatma Gandhi. His education included doctoral studies in systematic theology at Boston University between 1951 and 1955. In these years, King delivered sermons at a number of churches in the city, acquiring a reputation as a powerful and charismatic preacher. It was here that he gained inspiration and direction from the Reverend Howard Thurman, the first black chaplain at Boston University, and where he began dating his future wife, Coretta Scott, a student at the New England Conservatory of Music.

King's papers are among the treasures of Boston University's manuscript collections. His major books were collected sermons and essays, such as *Stride Toward Freedom* (1958), *Why We Can't Wait* (1964), *and Where Do We Go From Here?* (1967).

Martin Luther King, Jr.

Directly across the Common, along Boylston Street, are two other notable sites. In a lodging house on the road once called Carver Street (now part of Charles Street South), **Edgar Allan Poe** was born in January 1809. Later that summer, Poe and his parents — both professional actors — moved to New York, but the young Edgar returned to Boston in 1827 in search of literary fame.

One of Poe's eerie tales, "The Cask of Amontillado," had its origins in Boston. According to Edward Rowe Snow — known and loved for his storytelling histories of the Boston Harbor Islands — a sword duel took place on Castle Island, in South Boston, on Christmas Day, 1817. In the brief encounter, a young Robert Massie was slain by the fort bully, Lieutenant Gustavus Drane ("Captain Green" in Snow's stories). Enraged by Massie's death, the other soldiers got Drane drunk, hauled him into the fort's dungeon, chained him down, and sealed up the vault. Soon after, a memorial was erected on the site for their slain friend, Massie. Ten years later, under the name Edwin A. Perry, Poe enlisted in the 1st Massachusetts Heavy Artillery at Castle Island. He saw the monument, heard the tale — apocryphal though it may have been — and the rest, as they say, is literary history.

Edgar Allan Poe

In 1989 a plaque was put up at 176 Boylston Street commemorating Poe. Poe had a love-hate relationship with Boston and often referred to it as "Frogpondium," after the frog pond on the Common. A comment in his *Broadway Journal* typifies his ambivalent feelings: *We like Boston. We were born there — and perhaps it is just as well not to mention that we are heartily ashamed of the fact. The Bostonians are very well in their way. Their hotels are bad. Their pumpkin pies are delicious. Their poetry is not so good. Their Common is not a common thing — and the duck pond might answer — if its answer could be heard for the frogs.*

Several doors to the left of Poe's plaque is the gracious **Colonial Theater**, at 106 Boylston. This site was one home of the Boston Public Library before it moved to Back Bay in 1895. The blocks behind and next to the Colonial are considered Boston's Theater District. The best history of playhouses, plays, playwriting, and actors in Boston is *Broadway Down East* (1978), an excellent book by the acknowledged dean of Boston theater critics, Elliot Norton.

Continuing down Beacon Street, with the Common on your left, you are on the slope of **Beacon Hill**. The beautiful, exclusive homes on the beautiful, exclusive streets of Beacon Hill have long sheltered nationally known writers. Louisa May Alcott, Henry David Thoreau, and Sylvia Plath, as well as the historians William Cooper Nell, Henry Adams, Francis Parkman, and William Hickling Prescott are among the many authors who lived here. It was on Charles Street, at the base of

Harriet Beecher Stowe, 1868

Beacon Hill, that Annie Fields and Sarah Orne Jewett held their literary salons, and on Joy Street, on the north slope of the Hill, that the African Meeting House provided a platform for antislavery speeches, rallies, and writings. Harriet Beecher Stowe was a frequent guest at both places.

Now you can either follow the main route of the Literary Trail, down Beacon Street, or turn "Off the Beaten Path" for a walking tour of Beacon Hill.

Beacon Hill

APPROXIMATE TIME: 1 HOUR

Boston's first English settler was also the first colonist to inhabit the area now known as Beacon Hill. **The Reverend William Blackstone** (1595–1675), an Anglican expatriate from Robert Gorges's exploratory party of 1623, became a happy hermit here by 1625. The eccentric Blackstone contentedly rode about on his white bull and read from his collection of close to two hundred books — what might be called Boston's first library. Shortly after he invited John Winthrop's Massachusetts Bay Colony to share the Shawmut Peninsula, Blackstone left for less congested spaces.

The poet and novelist Conrad Aiken immortalized Blackstone in his 1947 poem "The Kid":

Where now he roves, by wood or swamp whatever,
the always restless, always moving on,
his books burned, and his own book lost forever,
under the cold stars of New England, gone,

scholar who loved, and therefor left, the most,

secret and solitary, no Indian-giver,
who to his own cost played the generous host,
and asked adventurers across his river:

what would he make of us, if he could see,
after so many tides have ringed this coast,
what manner of men his children's children be,
to welcome home his still inquisitive ghost?

Meanwhile, Winthrop and his colonists renamed the peninsula Trimount, then Boston, and began creating systems to protect their young settlement from invasion. One such system was a warning beacon set on the top of the tallest hill. If intruders were spotted in the harbor, a bucket filled with tar was set aflame and hiked to the top of a pole.

This area of Boston still bears names that reflect the days of early settlement. The hill, and later the street, were called Beacon. Trimount became Tremont. And one of the lesser of the three hills, Mount Vernon,

Beacon Hill Tour
1 Former Little, Brown and Company headquarters
2 Beacon Press
3 Mount Vernon Street
   Nichols House Museum (55)
   Henry Adams house (57)
   Thomas Bailey Aldrich house (59)
4 Club of Odd Volumes
5 Joy Street/Smith Court
   Abiel Smith School (46 Joy)
   William Cooper Nell house (3 Smith Court)
   African Meeting House (8 Smith Court)
6 Pinckney Street
   Henry David Thoreau lodgings (4)
   Louise Imogen Guiney house (16)
   Alcott family lodgings (20)
   Louisa May Alcott lodgings (43 and 81)
   Old Phillips School (65 Anderson)

   Thomas Bailey Aldrich house (84)
   F. O. Matthiessen House (87)
7 Louisburg Square
   John Gorham Palfrey house (5)
   William Dean Howells house (4 and 16)
   M. A. DeWolfe Howe house (16)
   Louisa May and Bronson Alcott house (10)
   Archibald MacLeish house
8 J. P. Marquand house
9 Lucretia Peabody Hale house
10 Site of James and Annie Fields house
11 Charles Street Meeting House
12 Henry and Alice James apartment
13 Samuel Eliot Morison house
14 Robert Frost house
15 Sylvia Plath apartment
16 Francis Parkman house
17 Julia Ward Howe house (13)
    Radical Club (13)

was immortalized by a street name as well as by the Mount Vernon Proprietors, the group of five entrepreneurs who developed and built up this land at the end of the eighteenth century.

Begin your walking tour where Joy Street runs into Beacon, across from the Common. You'll note that the street first ascends the south slope, then descends the north slope of the Hill. The line between these slopes, not terribly apparent today, was significant for most of the nineteenth and early twentieth centuries.

While prosperous white families bought land and built elegant homes on the sunny southern slope, overlooking Boston Common, their hired hands and unsightly outbuildings — servants, housemaids, stable boys, and stables — were often relegated to the congested, far less glorious back side of Beacon Hill. That north-south slope division also explains why so many persecuted and impoverished Eastern European Jewish immigrants and African Americans were able to live on Beacon Hill and in the adjacent West End through the nineteenth and into the early twentieth century.

In 1909, the house at 34 Beacon Street, at the corner of Joy, became the headquarters of **Little, Brown and Company.** Begun in 1837, when Charles C. Little and James Brown established Little & Brown, this publishing house was Houghton Mifflin Company's chief rival in Boston for several generations. Though it built a strong foundation with law books, Little & Brown won its first real literary acclaim with the nineteenth-century historic works of Francis Parkman.

Like Houghton Mifflin — whose offices were for many years at 4, then 2, Park Street — Little, Brown spent much of the twentieth century overlooking Boston Common. Although in different locations, both houses remain major international players to this day. Little, Brown is now part of the Time Warner conglomerate and has moved its editorial offices to New York.

As you walk up Joy to the corner of Mount Vernon Street, notice 41 Mount Vernon on the right. Once part of Little, Brown, it is currently the home of **Beacon Press.** Founded in 1932, Beacon was considered a religious publishing house, owing to its connection with the Unitarian (later, Unitarian-Universalist) Church. By its second decade, however, Beacon had become more diverse and garnered general praise and notice. In the 1970s, it joined the national controversy when it published the Pentagon Papers.

Take a short left onto Mount Vernon to view three impressive houses on the right.

At 55 Mount Vernon is the **Rose Standish Nichols House** and **Nichols House Museum**. A pacifist, pioneering garden designer, and international traveler, **Rose Standish Nichols** (1872–1964) left posterity a beautiful home designed by Charles Bulfinch that offers a glimpse of the old Beacon Hill mansions. An originator of the Beacon Hill Reading Club and one of the founders of the Women's International League for Peace and Freedom, Nichols wrote three outstanding volumes about landscape architecture: *English Pleasure Gardens, Italian Pleasure Gardens,* and *Spanish and Portuguese Gardens.*

Next door, at 57 Mount Vernon, is the boyhood home of **Henry Adams** (1838–1918). A member of *the* Adams family of Massachusetts — which had already produced one framer of the Declaration of Independence, two U.S. presidents, and assorted congressmen, diplomats, and political crusaders — Adams was something of a lost

Henry Adams, sketch by Samuel Lawrence

soul. The work for which he is best known, *The Education of Henry Adams* (1907), explores his feelings of miseducation and his sense that he was snubbed by Boston society.

During the 1870s, Adams abandoned his thoughts of a career in politics and became an assistant professor of medieval history at Harvard while editing the *North American Review.* Restless, he moved to Washington, D.C., where he wrote the anonymous novel *Democracy* (1880), satirizing political corruption in the capital.

Happily married to his beloved Marian Hooper in 1872,

Adams fell into disarray following her suicide in 1885. Extended trips to the Far East, the South Pacific, and Europe allowed him to sidestep his sorrows periodically and to devote himself to his nine-volume *History of the United States During the Administrations of Thomas Jefferson and James Madison* (1889–1891) and other scholarly works.

Despite much appreciation of his work, Adams's self-analysis was decidedly grim: *I want to look like an American Voltaire or Gibbon, but am slowly settling down to be a third-rate Boswell hunting for a Dr. Johnson.*

Thomas Bailey Aldrich (1836–1907), editor of the *Atlantic Monthly* from 1881 to 1890, moved to the townhouse at 59 Mount Vernon in 1885 and remained here until his death. Though born in New Hampshire and raised in New Hampshire, New Orleans, and New York, Aldrich began his relationship with Boston when Ticknor & Fields published his book of poems *Blue and Gold* in 1865. An editing job at the illustrated journal *Every Saturday* brought him to the city that same year.

When not editing *Every Saturday* and the *Atlantic Monthly*, Aldrich was a journalist, poet, short story writer, and novelist. His best-known work was the semi-autobiographical *Story of a Bad Boy* (1873).

In *Memories of a Hostess*, Annie Fields recalled the curly-haired Aldrich as a bright, refreshing companion and curious fellow: *He is a queer, witty creature. When the railroad dropped us at Green Lodge station . . . we found him sitting on a corner of the platform where he said he had been "listening to the bullfrog tune his violin. He had been twanging at one string a long time!" Aldrich was in an ecstasy of delight, and in truth it was a day to put the most untuned spirit into tune.*

Farther down the street, 77 Mount Vernon is the mansion housing the **Club of Odd Volumes**, established in 1887 by a group of Boston men interested in writing and collecting books. Its Saturday lunches continue to this day for those interested in all facets of scholarship.

Incidentally, 48 Mount Vernon was the address William Dean Howells chose for the fictional Coreys — the proper Bostonians who were duly shocked when poor Silas Lapham became inebriated at a dinner party in *The Rise of Silas Lapham* (1885).

Returning from Mount Vernon to Joy Street, begin your walk down Beacon Hill's north slope. On your left, 36A is a renovated carriage house and a well-maintained vestige of horse-and-carriage days. Turn left into Smith Court to see three important landmarks in Boston's black literary history.

At the corner, 46 Joy Street is the old **Abiel Smith School**. Opened in 1835 as the first public school in Boston to educate African-American children, it became the battleground for the desegregation of Boston schools — a battle won, in theory at least, by 1855. Judge Lemuel Shaw presided over the original 1849 court case; he was the father-in-law of Herman Melville. Under renovation during 1999, the building is the headquarters of both the Boston African American National Historic Site and the Museum of Afro American History.

African Meeting House

The double house at 3 Smith Court was once the home of the black historian, writer, abolitionist, and integrationist **William Cooper Nell** (1816–1874). The son of an early antislavery advocate and a close colleague of William Lloyd Garrison's, Nell worked his way up from errand boy to journalist and office manager at Garrison's abolitionist newspaper, *The Liberator*. Nell's most important book, *The Colored Patriots of the American Revolution* (1855), chronicled the accomplishments of African Americans that had not been previously documented. Its introduction was written by Harriet Beecher Stowe, the best-selling author of *Uncle Tom's Cabin* (1852).

The **African Meeting House**, at 8 Smith Court, is the oldest African-American church built by free black labor still standing on its original site. Created as a place of worship, community center, and schoolroom for the Hill's growing population of free blacks, the African Meeting House became both a symbol of hope and a landmark in black history. Most of the major abolitionist orators, activists, and writers spoke and rallied here in the decades before the Civil War. Prominent among the African-American speakers were **Frederick Douglass** (ca. 1817–1895) and **Maria W. Stewart** (1803–1879).

Douglass was born Frederick Bailey, a Maryland slave, in 1817. When one of his early owners, Mrs. Hugh Auld, began teaching him to read, she was ordered by her husband to stop: "If [Frederick] learns to read," he warned, "it will forever unfit him to be a slave. He should know nothing but the will of his master, and learn to obey it." Auld did find it in his heart to teach his slave to be a ship's caulker — a trade that came in handy when Frederick escaped fom slavery and Baltimore in 1838 and moved to Massachusetts with his wife.

Shortly after his arrival, he changed his name to Douglass to make himself more difficult to trace. He also discovered *The Liberator*, William Lloyd Garrison's abolitionist newspaper, which led to his involvement in antislavery society activities. A powerful orator, Douglass spoke in pulpits ranging from the African Meeting House, Faneuil Hall, and Tremont Temple in Boston to halls throughout the British Isles. He published his own antislavery newspaper, *North Star*, and wrote three autobiographies, the best known of which is *Narrative of the Life of Frederick Douglass* (1845).

Douglass also worked at the African Meeting House to enlist soldiers for the 54th Massachusetts volunteers, who fought under Colonel Robert Gould Shaw. Two of Douglass's sons were among the first recruits.

In 1987, the Boston writer and historian Marilyn Richardson recalled another significant voice associated with the African Meeting House in *Maria W. Stewart: America's First Black Woman Political Writer*. Stewart was an influential black activist, militant abolitionist, and defender of women's rights, and is now recognized as a significant

Frederick Douglass

The Liberator, masthead, 1859

forerunner of more familiar people like Frederick Douglass and Sojourner Truth.

Stewart was the first American woman, black or white, to lecture publicly on political themes — and possibly the first black American to espouse women's rights in public. Her speeches became some of *The Liberator*'s earliest antislavery articles, and her religious meditations and lectures were compiled in pamphlets and volumes of collected works. Among her most compelling exhortations was a call for action to her black sisterhood in the essay "Religion and the Pure Principles of Morality": *Ye daughters of Africa, awake! Awake! Arise! No longer sleep nor slumber, but distinguish yourselves. Show forth to the world that ye are endowed with noble and exalted faculties.*

Walk back up Joy Street and turn right on Pinckney. On the left is 4 Pinckney, an apartment where **Henry David Thoreau** once lived.

A little farther on the right, 15 Pinckney is one of several locations where **Elizabeth Palmer Peabody** held her kindergarten classes. Linked by family, friendship, and her own lifework to transcendentalism, major nineteenth-century authors, and innovative educators, Peabody combined her idealism with solid notions of educational reform in advocating a national system of kindergartens. Peabody, who also ran the influential Elizabeth Peabody Book Shop on West Street, is popularly known as the founder of the American kindergarten movement.

The Irish-American poet **Louise Imogen Guiney** (1861–1920) once lived at 16 Pinckney. A protégée and friend of Annie Fields and Sarah Orne Jewett, Guiney was an impoverished daughter of an Irish immigrant who grew into an established poet, essayist, and literary scholar producing more than thirty books in her lifetime. Her most distinguished poetry and prose collections were *A Roadside Harp* (1893) and *Patrins* (1897). Heralded as "the Laureate of the Lost," Guiney was also committed to gaining recognition for obscure seventeenth-century Catholic English poets. Despite growing praise and admiration, her books sold poorly, forcing her to take a variety of jobs, including that of cataloger at the Boston Public Library. Her fans and friends came to include such contemporaries as Oliver Wendell Holmes, Jr., Thomas Bailey Aldrich, and Thomas Wentworth Higginson.

Though **Louisa May Alcott** usually had at least one home in Concord, she often maintained a pied-à-terre in Boston. A plaque on 20 Pinckney notes that Alcott was a little girl when her family rented this apartment. Alcott also rented rooms at 43 and 81 Pinckney — the latter overlooking Louisburg Square. Though Louisa had loved the town of Concord as a child, she felt far more at home in the city during her adult years.

At the corner of Pinckney and Anderson is 65 Anderson, with 1824 carved above its front door. Built as the **Phillips School** —

one of Boston's finest centers for educating white children — it became one of the city's first integrated schools after the desegregation ruling of 1855.

Thomas Bailey Aldrich, whom we met on Mount Vernon Street, made his first Boston home at 84 Pinckney.

Professor **F. O. (Francis Otto) Matthiessen** (1902–1950) lived at 87 Pinckney, also overlooking Louisburg Square. A Rhodes Scholar and graduate of Yale and Harvard, Matthiessen was a brilliant, religious man and incisive literary critic. He was also an influential teacher at both his alma maters and established the academic discipline now known as American Studies. Among his books are *Sarah Orne Jewett* (1929), *The Achievement of T. S. Eliot* (1935), *The James Family* (1947), and *American Renaissance* (1941). Politically liberal and openly gay, Matthiessen was the long-time companion of painter Russell Cheney until the latter's death in 1945. During the McCarthy era, Matthiessen was persecuted for both his political opinions and his personal life. He committed suicide in 1950.

The lovely private neighborhood lodged peacefully between Pinckney and Mount Vernon streets is **Louisburg** (pronounced Lewisberg) **Square**.

Louisburg Square

Palfrey's five-volume *History of New England* (1858–1890) was a formidable work, well used and respected in his time.

Two of the even-numbered homes on the slope below the green — numbers 4 and 16 — were rented

Built between 1833 and 1847 as one of Boston's finest and most exclusive residential areas, it remains to this day an urban oasis, replete with a manicured park surrounded by an iron fence and handsome Greek Revival houses.

The strip of homes on the upper slope of the square has odd numbers. The Unitarian clergyman **John Gorham Palfrey** (1796–1881), who wrote many religious books, once lived at number 5. Palfrey is best remembered for owning and editing the *North American Review*, a prestigious journal started in 1811 by the founders of the Boston Athenaeum. (The *Review*, as well as the *Atlantic Monthly*, were later purchased by James T. Fields of the Old Corner Bookstore.)

by **William Dean Howells**, a novelist and editor of the *Atlantic Monthly*, between 1882 and 1884. Howells often discussed life and literature with colleague Henry James at number 16, and began writing his masterwork, *The Rise of Silas Lapham* (1885) there. We'll meet Howells again on the Literary Trail in Cambridge.

Number 16 was also the last home of the editor, biographer, poet, and antiquarian **M. A. (Mark Antony) DeWolfe Howe** (1864–1960), who published an astonishing number of books on New England and Boston. Among his titles were *Boston Common: Scenes from Four Centuries* (1910), *Letters of Charles Eliot Norton* (1913), *The Atlantic Monthly and Its Makers* (1919),

Memories of a Hostess (1922), and the Pulitzer Prize–winning *Barrett Wendell and His Letters* (1924).

His daughter, Helen Howe (1905–1975), chronicled Boston's nineteenth-century literary life in *The Gentle Americans* (1965).

The most prominent literary figures on Louisburg Square were surely **Louisa May Alcott** (1832–1888) and her father, the transcendentalist **A. Bronson Alcott** (1799–1888), who lived at 10 Louisburg Square from 1885 to 1888. Though long associated with Orchard House in Concord — where the family lived for almost two decades — the Alcotts were transient tenants at best, often forced to move when Bronson's progressive schools invariably failed. Especially after the success of *Little Women* (1868), Louisa proved a far better provider than her father.

Louisburg Square was the last home for both Louisa and Bronson. They both died in the spring of 1888, within two days of each other. Curiously, both father and daughter had been born on the same day — November 29 — Bronson in 1799 and Louisa in 1832.

More contemporary authors who have lived on Louisburg Square include **Robin Cook** (b. 1940), the author of the medical thrillers *Coma, Brain, Fever,* and *Outbreak,* and the Pulitzer Prize–winning poet and playwright **Archibald MacLeish** (1892–1982).

After serving in World War I and graduating from Harvard Law School (1919), Archibald MacLeish made his name in the world of letters, in time becoming a Boylston Professor of Rhetoric and Oratory at Harvard (1949–1962). In between several exceptional posts — including Librarian of Congress and Assistant Secretary of State under Franklin D. Roosevelt — MacLeish passed prolifically through periods of experimental and socially progressive poetry, plays, prose, and verse drama. He was awarded Pulitzer Prizes in poetry for *Conquistador* (1932) and *Collected Poems, 1917–1952* (1952) and in drama for *J.B.* (1958), a modern retelling of the biblical trials of Job.

Countless writers have immortalized Louisburg Square,

A poem should not mean
But be.

— Archibald MacLeish,
Ars Poetica (1926)

---

including **Jean Stafford** (1915–1979), who captured its essence in her first novel, *Boston Adventure* (1944): *Her house was not far; its front windows faced Louisburg Square and here, as if it were an oasis chosen to delight the eyes of some favored heavenly power, the sun, hidden elsewhere by the city's smoke, shone brilliantly on white doorways and their brass trimmings.*

A novelist and short story writer, Stafford was born in California and raised in Colorado. *Boston Adventure* was the most popular of her novels, which included *The Catherine Wheel* (1952), *A Winter's Tale* (1954), and *Bad Characters* (1964). She also wrote an account of the mother of Lee Harvey Oswald, *A Mother in History* (1966).

Stafford was the first (and very unhappy) wife of Robert Lowell, who was raised at 91 Revere Street, just two blocks away. That address was immortalized in Lowell's satiric prose memoir of the same name in his confessional *Life Studies* (1959).

Return to Pinckney Street and follow it down to West Cedar. Several doors down on the right is 43 West Cedar, where **J. P. (John Phillips) Marquand** (1893–1960) once lived. His first

> Marriage . . . is a damnably serious business, particularly around Boston.
>
> — J. P. Marquand, *The Late George Apley* (1937)

books were popular romances and detective stories; the Japanese detective Mr. Moto was one of his most memorable characters. Marquand's greatest novel, however, was *The Late George Apley*, an insightful tale that gently satirized Boston's Brahmins and won the Pulitzer Prize in 1937.

It seems that Marquand was insecure when he first began writing *Apley*. After a friend in New York turned down the early manuscript, he asked Alfred McIntyre — another friend and for years the head of Little, Brown — for a quick evaluation. "John, I think it is swell," McIntyre responded. "I can't tell you whether it will sell more than 2,000 copies — it may be too highly specialized. But by all means, go ahead with it!"

Turn left on Revere Street and go down to Charles Street, at the base of the Hill. Due to modern alterations, the street numbers here differ from their nineteenth-century order. Keeping that in mind, walk along the right side of the street.

Lucretia Peabody Hale (1820–1900), a member of the illustrious Hale family — and the sister of Edward Everett Hale — lived at 127 Charles. A political progressive, Lucretia worked for women's rights and educational and social reform. Once a student in Elizabeth Peabody's school, she later helped start kindergartens and vacation schools while serving as one of the first two women on the Boston School Committee. A contributor to the *Atlantic* from 1858, Hale is best known for her amusing collection of sketches about Bostonians' penchant for self-improvement, *The Peterkin Papers* (1880).

Across the street, near the Charles Street Garage, stood that legendary gathering place of literary greats, 148 Charles Street. In "The American Scene" (1907), Henry James described "the waterside museum" of **James** and **Annie Fields** with appropriate awe: *Here, behind the effaced, anonymous door was the little ark of the modern deluge, here still the long drawing-room that looks over the water and towards the sunset, with a seat for every visiting shade, from far-away Thackeray down, and relics and tokens so thick on its walls as to make it positively, in all the town, the votive temple to memory.*

When James T. Fields of the Old Corner Bookstore moved here in 1856, the building was listed as 37 Charles Street; a decade later, it was renumbered 148. Regardless, its aura was absolutely stunning and the literary connections seemingly infinite. A typical encounter was remembered by Annie Fields in *Memories of a Hostess* (1922): *Dr. [Oliver Wendell] Holmes and his wife and Mr. [John Greenleaf] Whittier dined here. The talk was free, totally free from all feeling of constraint, as it could not have been had another person been present. Whittier says he is afraid of strangers, and Dr. Holmes is never more delightful than under just such auspices.*

Though James T. Fields died in 1881, the Charles Street salons did not die with him. Quite the contrary. Immediately after his death, a talented young writer from South Berwick, Maine, **Sarah Orne Jewett** (1849–1909), became Annie Fields's constant companion in a relationship that lasted the rest of their lives. Jewett's elegant and keenly observed stories of New England country life included *Deephaven* (1877), *Old Friends and New* (1879), *A Country Doctor* (1884), and her masterpiece, *The*

Country of the Pointed Firs (1896).

As a young teenager in rural Maine, Jewett was inspired by Harriet Beecher Stowe's *Pearl of Orr's Island.* Convinced that sophisticated Bostonians vacationing in Maine did not appreciate the area's natural surroundings and simple, grand people, she determined to remedy that vision. At the age of nineteen, Jewett entered an illustrious literary circle when her first story was published in the *Atlantic Monthly*, thus beginning her lifelong association with the magazine and her vital connection to the Fields family. (In 1869, James T. Fields was still editor of the *Atlantic*.)

Committed in what was known as a "Boston marriage," Annie Adams Fields and Sarah Orne Jewett were in the compa-ny of similar women of the late Victorian era. Alice James and Katharine Loring were life partners, as were the sculptor Anne Whitney and Adeline Manning, Amy Lowell and Ada Dwyer Russell, and Katherine Lee Bates (who wrote the lyrics to "America the Beautiful") and Katharine Coman. These liaisons — generally between wealthy professional women who could support themselves — were fairly well accepted by Boston society and treated as any other marriage.

Perhaps because of their strong female bond, the Fields-Jewett salons were particular magnets for women writers and artists. Among those in attendance was the young **Willa Cather** (1873–1947), who observed and adored Fields and Jewett in her charming book *Not Under Forty* (1922): *Mrs. Fields wore the widow's lavender which she never abandoned except for black velvet, with a scarf of Venetian lace on her hair. She was very slight and fragile in figure, with a great play of animation in her face and a delicate flush of pink on her cheeks. Like her friend Mrs. John Gardner, she had a skin which defied age. As for Miss Jewett — she looked very like the youthful picture of herself in the game of "Authors" I had played as*

Sarah Orne Jewett

a child, except that she was fuller in figure and a little grey. I do not at all remember what we talked about. Mrs. Brandeis asked that I be shown some of the treasures of the house, but I had no eyes for the treasures, I was too intent upon the ladies.

Turn around and head back toward the Common and the Public Garden. On the right, where Charles meets Mount Vernon, is 121 Mount Vernon.

Built in 1807 as a house of worship — a role it played for four consecutive congregations over 173 years — the **Charles Street Meeting House** was also a vibrant community center that witnessed meetings, educational forums, and spirited debates involving everyone from Sojourner Truth, Langston Hughes, Dr. Benjamin Spock, and leaders of the Beacon Hill Civic Association to members of feminist, gay, civil rights, arts, and peace groups. The modest display that grew into the Museum of Afro American History began here, as did the groundbreaking *Gay Community News,* the nation's oldest gay newspaper.

Before landfill separated the church from the river for several blocks, the Charles flowed up to the side of the brick meeting house, where River Street runs today. When nineteenth-century Baptists worshiped here, an underground opening on the river side apparently allowed baptism by immersion to take place inside the church *without* any fancy pumps or plumbing!

Continue walking down Mount Vernon to number 131, on your right, the home of **Henry James** and his sister, **Alice**, for a brief period after their parents died. Henry also lived in some rooms at 102 Mount Vernon. The Jameses will reappear in the Cambridge segment of the Literary Trail.

Stop at the corner of Brimmer and Mount Vernon streets. The ivy-covered brick house on the left, 44 Brimmer, was the boyhood home of **Samuel Eliot Morison** (1887–1976). Esteemed as a professor of American history at Harvard, an editor of the *New England Quarterly,* the official historian of the U.S. Navy during World War II, and a maritime historian par excellence, Morison's life here is best described in his brief yet eloquent memoir, *One Boy's Boston, 1887–1901* (1962).

At the turn of the last century, writes Morison, this area at the base of Beacon Hill was filled with sights, sounds, and smells quite different from those of today: *Almost the entire square between the backs of Beacon, River and Mt. Vernon Streets, and the river, was occupied by stables big and little — livery stables, which let out "sea-going" hacks and coupes; boarding and baiting stables, where gentlemen who drove in from the suburbs behind fast trotters left their rigs during the day; club stables where individuals could board one or two horses; dozens of private stables. Chestnut Street between Charles and the river was called "Horse-Chestnut Street" in derision. . . . On Lime Street, there were at least two blacksmith shops, where the cheerful ringing of hammer on anvil could be heard from 7 A.M. to late afternoon. There was Chauncy Thomas's carriage factory on Lower Chestnut Street, where beautiful sleighs, victorias, broughams and other horse-drawn vehicles were built; Frederic J. Fisher, the famous body designer for automobiles, there had his training. . . . My descendants will find it hard to believe that I once kept a horse at the Beacon Club Stable . . . and that even after becoming Professor Hart's assistant at Harvard I would combine business with pleasure by riding my grey gelding "Blanco" to Cambridge, tying him to a tree in the Yard, and loading the saddlebags with students' papers that had to be corrected.*

Return to the corner of Charles Street and ascend Mount Vernon. As you turn right onto Willow Street, notice 88 Mount Vernon on the corner. **Robert Frost** — whom we'll encounter again in Cambridge — moved here in 1939.

Follow Willow Street to number 9, which faces the cobblestones of Acorn Street, perhaps the most photographed road in the city. Created as a back alley and filled with inexpensive rowhouses for servants and the less affluent, Acorn Street is now a scenic delight. Tourists often aim their cameras up the street, apparently smitten with this tiny slice of old Boston.

In 1958, **Sylvia Plath** (1932–1963) moved to an apartment at 9 Willow while taking Robert Lowell's seminar at Boston University. Among her fellow students there were the poets Anne Sexton and George Starbuck. Throughout her formal education — which included public schools in Winthrop and Wellesley, Massachusetts, followed by a scholarship at Smith College — Plath showed an aptitude for writing poetry and short stories. She also had a tendency toward anxiety, depression, paranoia, and suicide attempts, and she underwent electroconvulsive therapy at

McLean Hospital in Belmont, Massachusetts, after her junior year of college.

Plath's depressed state had many sources, including the death of her father when she was eight, and a troubled marriage to Ted Hughes, Britain's poet laureate. The darkness she lived in provided the material for much of her work, including her stunning novel, *The Bell Jar* (1963), first published under the pseudonym of Victoria Lewis. Her suicide in 1963, at the age of thirty, was prophetically alluded to in works like "Lady Lazarus" (1962):

Dying
Is an art, like everything else.
I do it exceptionally well.
I do it so it feels like hell.

Many of Plath's intensely personal poems, prose, and letters were published in posthumous collections, including *Ariel* (1966), *Crossing the Water* (1971), *Johnny Panic and the Bible of Dreams* (1977), and *Letters Home* (1975). Her *Collected Poems* (1981) won a Pulitzer Prize.

Plath's classmate **Anne Sexton** (1928–1974) is generally considered her soulmate as well. Though Anne Harvey of Newton, Massachusetts, had written some poetry early in life, she wandered in other directions for several years — marrying Alfred M. Sexton II at nineteen, working as a fashion model and librarian, and raising two daughters. Discovering her talent for poetry became a personal salvation for Sexton, a way to ease her increasing anguish and perhaps ward off nervous breakdowns and suicide attempts. Beginning with her work in Robert Lowell's seminars, Sexton produced an impressive, self-exploratory body of work, including *To Bedlam and Part Way Back* (1960), *All My Pretty Ones* (1962), *The Death Notebooks* (1974), and the posthumously published *45 Mercy Street* (1976). Her accolades include a Pulitzer Prize, a National Book Award, and a Guggenheim Fellowship.

At forty-five, Sexton was found dead in an idling car in her Weston garage. Her fellow poet and friend Maxine Kumin, with whom Sexton wrote several

Anne Sexton

children's books, explained to the press: "Life had a depressing effect on [Anne].... Other times there were little notes or little warnings left about . . . but this time, no signs at all."

As Willow ends, take a right diagonal over to 50 Chestnut Street. As noted by its National Historic Landmark plaque, **Francis Parkman** (1823–1893) lived in this townhouse between 1865 and 1893. Born in Boston to a prominent family and educated at Boston Latin School, Harvard College, and Harvard Law School, Parkman was destined to become America's preeminent nineteenth-century historian. Despite chronic ill health — a nervous condition, severe vision impairment, and general exhaustion — he longed to write a "history of the American forest." Hence, at twenty-three, he and his cousin Quincy Adams Shaw (the brother of the future Civil War colonel Robert Gould Shaw) began an ambitious and rugged journey from St. Louis, Missouri, to Wyoming. That trip, which included months spent with frontiersmen, pioneer settlers, and Native American tribes, culminated in Parkman's highly regarded work, *The Oregon Trail* (1849).

Despite the popularity of his

> I would like a simple life yet all night I am laying poems away in a long box.
> — Anne Sexton, *The Ambition Bird* (1973)

book, the year took its toll on the Parkman family. In the late fall of 1849, Francis's brother George was murdered, dissected, and burned in a Harvard Medical School oven by John White Webster, a faculty member. The bizarre investigation and sensational trial that followed mortified the Parkman family and intrigued the world (including Charles Dickens, who requested a visit to the murder site on his subsequent American reading tour). Among those who testified at the trial was Oliver Wendell Holmes. The judge was Lemuel Shaw, the father-in-law of Herman Melville.

Meanwhile, Francis Parkman's vision continued to deteriorate. With the assistance of readers and an instrument that helped him write with his eyes shut, Parkman — a consummate storyteller — created engaging narratives for the rest of his life. Among his major books are *History of the Conspiracy of Pontiac* (1851), the partly autobiographical *Vassall Morton* (1856), and the seven-volume *France and England in the New World* (1865–1892).

Walk up Chestnut Street and cross over to numbers 13–15. These dwellings, designed by Charles Bulfinch, were built by Madame Hepzibah Swan, the only woman in the group of entrepreneurs that developed Beacon Hill. One of America's first art collectors, Swan gave these houses as wedding gifts for her three daughters.

The most illustrious resident at 13 Chest-nut, however, was **Julia Ward Howe** (1819–1910), an abolitionist, poet, philanthropist, peace activist, feminist, social reformer, clubwoman, and mother of six. She also helped institute the original tribute to

---

AUTHOR / AUTHOR!

David McCullough on Francis Parkman

I can never pass by Number 50 Chestnut Street on Beacon Hill, once the home of Francis Parkman, without an inner nod of gratitude. Few have written history with such sweep and flavor as did Parkman. In his hands, history became literature. And for someone raised in Pittsburgh, as I was, at the confluence of the Allegheny and Monongahela Rivers, where in the mid-eighteenth century the titanic French and Indian War began, there is little to equal the power of Parkman's *France and England in North America,* volume one of which, *Pioneers of France in the New World*, first appeared in 1865.

But what I am especially and everlastingly indebted to the great man for is a single paragraph in an introduction he wrote for a later edition of the book. To me it's gospel.

Faithfulness to the truth of history involves more than a research, however patient and scrupulous, into special facts. Such facts may be detailed with the most minute exactness, and yet the narrative, taken as a whole, may be unmeaning or untrue. The narrator must seek to imbue himself with the life and spirit of the time. He must study events in their bearings near and remote; in the character, habits, and manners of those who took part in them. He must be, as it were, a sharer or a spectator of the action he describes.

mothers in America, the very practical and political Mother's Day for Peace, begun in 1872. (Howe's concept of Mother's Day — as a pacifist plea, for the world to stop killing their sons — failed to survive the century. It was replaced by today's more sentimental and commercial version, created by one Anna Jarvis and first officially celebrated in 1914.)

Julia Ward Howe, 1868

marching song, "John Brown's Body." Visiting Washington, D.C., during the early years of the Civil War, Howe heard the Bay State regiments singing "John Brown's Body" as they filed down the avenues. Caught by the music, she had her carriage chase after the soldiers. After borrowing the tune, the chorus, and an image or two, Howe's anthem was born — and published in the *Atlantic Monthly* in February 1862:

Howe was well regarded as an editor of the abolitionist periodical *Commonwealth* and for her many contributions to the *Woman's Journal.* Her books included collected poems, travel sketches, an 1883 biography of Margaret Fuller, and her own *Reminiscences* (1899). Her undying fame, however, is a result of her impassioned text to "The Battle Hymn of the Republic."

The tune behind Howe's lyrics began as a vintage camp song, "Say, Brothers, Will You Meet Us," which was copied by members of the 12th Massachusetts Infantry for their new

Mine eyes have seen the glory of the coming of the Lord;
He is trampling out the vintage where the grapes of wrath are stored;
He hath loosed the fateful lightning of His terrible, swift sword;
His truth is marching on.

Abraham Lincoln reportedly wept when he first heard the hymn. Mrs. Howe was paid five dollars by the *Atlantic.*

The Swan houses continued to harbor innovative thought

when Mrs. John T. Sargent moved in. From 1867 to 1880, 13 Chestnut served as a meeting place for the **Radical Club**, a group of daringly modern women and men that Sargent helped found. The liberal Unitarians who gathered here for discussion and debate included its former resident Julia Ward Howe as well as John Greenleaf Whittier, Ralph Waldo Emerson, and William Lloyd Garrison.

Continue up Mount Vernon and turn right onto Walnut. The main route of the Literary Trail resumes at the corner of Walnut and Beacon streets.

Return to the main route of the literary trail.

Immediately on your right is 39 Beacon Street, the Appleton family home, where Fannie married Henry Wadsworth Longfellow in 1843. They will be visited again on Brattle Street in Cambridge.

The museum at 55 Beacon, marked by a commemorative plaque, is the former home of the historian **William Hickling Prescott** (1796–1859). Like his fellow historian and neighbor Francis Parkman, Prescott was plagued by damaged eyesight. While studying at Harvard, he had been hit in the eye with a crust of bread. Despite one blind eye and a second one weakened by rheumatism, Prescott was determined to pursue a literary career. By 1826, however, he had shifted his sights from literary criticism to history.

For twelve years, Prescott committed all his faculties to writing a three-volume history of the reign of Ferdinand and Isabella of Spain.

Buoyed by its success, he went on to write *History of the Conquest of Mexico* (1843) and *History of the Conquest of Peru* (1847).

Among his international coterie of fans was Charles Dickens, whose letter to one Professor Felton was reprinted in James T. Fields's *Yesterdays With Authors* (1871): *I wrote to Prescott about his book, with which I was perfectly charmed. I think his description masterly, his style brilliant, his purpose manly and gallant always. The introductory account of Aztec civilization impressed me exactly as it impressed you. From beginning to end, the whole history is enchanting and full of genius.*

At the base of the hill is Charles Street. Near the Charles Street gate to the Public Garden is a statue of the writer, Unitarian minister, and reformer **Edward Everett Hale** (1822–1909), created by Bela Pratt and erected in 1913. Hale is best remembered for his classic patriotic tale, *The Man Without a Country*

(1863). Contemporaries, however, knew him also for his role at the turn of the twentieth century. On December 31, 1900, the seventy-eight-year-old Grand Old Man of Boston stood on the steps of the State House, faced a reverent and quiet crowd, and welcomed in the New Year — and new century — with a reading of Psalm 90.

A grandnephew of the Revolutionary War patriot Nathan Hale, Edward entered Harvard College at age thirteen and graduated four years later as class poet and a member of Phi Beta Kappa. His wife, Emily Baldwin Perkins, was a niece of Harriet Beecher Stowe's. When not writing, lecturing, and pursuing political causes — including world peace and abolition — Hale led Boston's South Congregational Church, where he preached for forty-three years.

Not far from the statue is one of the most popular pieces of outdoor sculpture in the city. *Mrs. Mallard and Her Eight Ducklings*, by the Newton artist Nancy Schön, was installed in 1987 to mark the 150th anniversary of the Public Garden. The shine on the bronze quackers' backs is from the countless children who lovingly play on them daily. The inspiration for this sculpture — **Robert McCloskey**'s (b. 1914) *Make Way for Ducklings!* — has been a children's classic since it was published in 1941.

McCloskey's simple, timeless story, set in Boston, chronicles the trials of Mr. and Mrs. Mallard as they search for a nice place to live with their ducklings. The author and illustrator studied mallard ducks in museums and libraries before creating his drawings. To perfect his understanding of their habits and movement, McCloskey bought four live ducks from a poultry dealer, took them to his apartment, and followed them about for weeks with Kleenex and sketchbook in hand.

Stories and verse for children and young teens have always been part of Boston's literary picture. The subject of children's literature is a book in itself, but it's easy to get a

glimpse of the role Bostonians played in this genre.

In the eighteenth century, Thomas Fleet (who may or may not have published Mother Goose's *Melodies*) did print the 1737 edition of *The New England Primer*. It was the first volume in which the children's prayer "Now I lay me down to sleep" was reproduced.

During the nineteenth century, Horatio Alger, Jr. (1832–1899), who was raised in Boston, made his rags-to-riches tales a part of American culture with dozens of redundant boys' books about Ragged Dick, Tattered Tom, and kindred spirits. Meanwhile, one of America's most popular series of "juveniles," the *Peter Parley* books, were prepared with the aid of Epes Sargent (1813–1880), the editor of the *Boston Transcript*, who also compiled school readers.

Louisa May Alcott's *Little Women*, of course, has been *the* classic for girls since its publication in 1868. Alcott, like many of her contemporaries, also contributed stories to nineteenth-century "juveniles," the term for magazines oriented to young people. The woman who helped save Alcott's Orchard House and The Wayside — Margaret Sidney, aka Harriett Mulford Stone Lothrop (1844–1924) — created her own children's favorites, the Five Little Peppers series.

Though Nathaniel Hawthorne

(1804–1864) and Henry Wadsworth Longfellow (1807–1882) are not known primarily as children's authors, many of their works were committed to memory by generations of American youth. Longfellow's poems are also credited with generating a pantheon of heroes — from Paul Revere and Hiawatha to Miles Standish and the Village Blacksmith — that had been lacking in American culture. At the end of the century, W. Gilbert Patten (1866–1945), under the name Burt L. Standish, turned out a series of books about Frank Merriwell, everyone's favorite star athlete, gentleman, and All-American boy.

By the twentieth century, children's books were well on their way to becoming big business. Many of these books were written in the Greater Boston area by authors who found the city a good setting. Among them are Kathryn Lasky (*I Have an Aunt on Marlborough Street*), Esther Forbes (*Johnny Tremain*), Margret and H. A. Rey (the *Curious George* books), E. B. White (*The Trumpet of the Swan*), Norma Farber (*As I Was Crossing Boston Common*), Lois Lowry (*Taking Care of Terrific*), Blair Lent (*Molasses Flood*), Ann Rinaldi (*Fifth of March*), Michael Emberley (*Ruby*), and Stephen Krensky (*Ghostly Business*).

The Public Garden, twenty-four beautifully landscaped acres, has been a source of joy for children for over a century. The Swan Boats in particular — started by Robert Paget in 1877 and still run by his descendants — have been the stuff of memory. **Elizabeth Bishop**, for example, was so impressed by her swan boat ride here in 1914, when she was three, that she vividly recalled it for the rest of her life.

Born in Worcester, Massachusetts, Bishop (1911–1979) was orphaned early in life and raised by a grandmother. Though she lived in this area for many years — first as a child, then later when hired to teach at Harvard and MIT — she also made her home in Nova Scotia, Greenwich Village, Key West, San Francisco, and Brazil. During her last year of study at Vassar College, Bishop met Marianne Moore, who became a significant mentor and friend, as did Robert Lowell more than a decade later.

First published in 1925 in an anthology introduced by Moore, Bishop was chosen Poet Laureate (then called Poetry Consultant at the Library of Congress) in 1949. By 1956 she had won the Pulitzer Prize for her book *Poems — North & South*, and by 1961 she was traveling down the Amazon River with Aldous Huxley. While her own true loves were women — most notably a Vassar classmate and a Brazilian aristocrat — Bishop was adored by Robert Lowell. In "For Elizabeth Bishop 4," Lowell mused on the

extraordinary length of time it took his friend to perfect her poems:

Do
you still hang your words in air, ten
*   years imperfect;*
joke-letters glued to your cardboard
*   posters, with gaps*
and empties for the unimaginable
*   phrase —*
unerring muse who scorns a less
*   casual friendship?*

You are now on the corner of Beacon and Arlington streets. The latter is the first of the alphabet streets — Arlington, Berkeley, Clarendon, Dartmouth, Exeter, Fairfield, Gloucester, and Hereford — which cross this beautiful old neighborhood of lengthy avenues, known as **Back Bay**. From colonial times through the early nineteenth century, it was indeed a bay, flooded by the Charles River during high tide, then reduced to odiferous mudflats when the tide ebbed. The space from the base of Boston Common through today's Public Garden was a beach, where residents swam, fished, and went boating, then clammed (or complained) when the tide was low.

The young Ben Franklin was among the many anglers here in the early eighteenth century. The British regulars who later camped out on the Common had yet another "angle": on the night of April 18, 1775, they boarded their

The Public Garden

Between 1857 and 1890, a major landfill project eliminated the old tidal flats, and the new real estate soon boasted fine homes and a variety of cultural institutions. One was the seminal *Atlantic Monthly*, which made its headquarters at 8 Arlington, on the corner of Arlington and Marlborough streets. Created at a Parker House gathering of the Saturday Club — a group that included Emerson, Longfellow, Lowell, and Holmes — the *Atlantic* began as a progressive Brahmin literary showcase, a self-proclaimed "journal of literature, politics, science, and the arts." Its first editors included James Russell Lowell (1857–1861), James T. Fields (1861–1871), and William Dean Howells (1871–1881).

boats for Cambridge, then marched on to Lexington and Concord while two lights flashed in the steeple of the Old North Church, warning patriots of their approach. Longfellow took poetic license in describing this episode in "Paul Revere's Ride" (1863):

One if by land, and two if by sea;
And I on the opposite shore will be,
Ready to ride and spread the alarm
Through every Middlesex village
and farm.

The "sea," of course, was the Charles River. And since there were no bridges, the Redcoats' only other route would have been the long stretch down today's Washington Street and through Roxbury.

When it first appeared in 1857, the *Atlantic* was boldly attempting to define and mold a distinctive American voice. From that time through the present it has been, among other things, a showcase for authors of note. Nathaniel Hawthorne sent in articles from the Civil War battlefront, and Julia Ward Howe offered her "Battle Hymn of the Republic." Felix Frankfurter made a plea on behalf of Sacco and Vanzetti, and Martin Luther King, Jr., presented a handwritten draft of his "Letter from Birmingham Jail." Many writers saw their first printed stories on the pages of the *Atlantic*, including Henry James, Mark Twain, Louise

---

AUTHOR / AUTHOR!

Robert Pinsky on Elizabeth Bishop

Boston's waterfront was only beginning its great rebirth when Elizabeth Bishop moved to her apartment on Lewis Wharf, in a splendidly restored former warehouse building of gray stone. The architect had left elegant reaches of exposed, ancient beams visible in the corridor, recalling the ships and shipping of the building's history, and in Elizabeth's apartment, among works of art and memorabilia from her long residence in Brazil, a carved figurehead maiden spread her wings. The building, reaching its massive, flinty rectangle out to Boston Harbor, seemed right for her restless, traveller's spirit. Her childhood was spent in Worcester and in Nova Scotia: the North End with its hermetic, winding streets opening suddenly to water views seemed to distill that ocean-saturated Canadian landscape and the domestic streets.

Before I knew her, before the Lewis Wharf days, Elizabeth Bishop lived for a time virtually in Harvard Square, in an apartment on Brattle Street. The building was marked by a small neon sign, cursive letters identifying it as the "Brattle Arms." The silly, old-fashioned name, a kind of vulnerable glamour or sophistication in the script, evoke for me another side of Bishop, her urban poems like "The Man-Moth" and "Varick Street." This side of her, utterly non-academic, urbane and unpedantic, seemed to belong in the North End, but when she was in Cambridge she made it that much less a mere college town, that much more part of the great world of sights, tastes, sounds, smells and textures — the world well represented by the coziness and adventure of a harborside.

Erdrich, Sue Miller, and Bobbie Ann Mason. In 1989, the *Atlantic* moved to Boylston Street, then to its current home, 77 North Washington.

Just around the corner from the old *Atlantic,* at 5 Commonwealth Avenue, is the house built in 1912 for Walter C. Baylies, a textile manufacturer. Now the Boston Center for Adult Education, it sponsors a broad spectrum of courses, includ-ing writing classes, seminars, and lectures by noted authors, poets, and journalists. In the 1950s, for example, the poet John Holmes (1904–1962) taught a writing class here to a group that included Anne Sexton.

Beacon Street itself was called "the sunny street that holds the sifted few" by one resident, Oliver Wendell Holmes. Few private owners can afford these grand mansions today, though, many of them have been bought by educational institutions. On this stretch of Beacon, you'll find doors marked Fisher College and Emerson College.

Still, the well-preserved **Gibson House**, at 137 Beacon, is a museum that gives visitors a glimpse of opulent Victorian Boston at its finest. The first row house (1859) on the south side of Beacon between Arlington and Berkeley streets, the Gibson House is a fine example of the Back Bay during Boston's literary Golden Age. While the facade of the house features beautiful work by Edward Clarke Cabot — the same architect who designed the Boston Athenaeum — the interior offers nineteenth-century books, furnishings, and technological innovations, as well as paintings, photographs, and even daguerreotypes of the historic Warren family.

Since 1974 the house has served as the headquarters of the New England Chapter of the Victorian Society. It became a museum thanks to the vision of Charles Hammond Gibson, Jr., the colorful bon vivant who was known as much as a horticulturist, writer, and poet as he was for shocking proper Bostonians with his eccentric mannerisms and dress.

Most people associate the legendary art collector and patron **Isabella Stewart Gardner** with her palatial home in the Fens, but a plaque near 150 Beacon, on the right side of the street, marks the site of her first home in Boston. Years before she built Fenway Court — now the Gardner Museum — the charming and controversial "Mrs. Jack" lived at 152 Beacon, between Berkeley and Clarendon streets. After the deaths of her only son, her husband, and a variety of relatives, Gardner was left with a lot of sorrow — and a lot of money.

She also had a great deal of good sense and surrounded herself with Boston's cultural elite as well as some of its most celebrated Bohemians. When not mixing with the likes of Henry James, Henry Adams, James McNeil Whistler, John Singer Sargent, and Charles Eliot Norton, Gardner was busy

> The continuity of glass constituted a kind of exposure, within and without, and gave [Beacon] street an appearance of an enormous corridor, in which the public and the private were familiar and intermingled. But it was all very cheerful and commodious, and seemed to speak of diffused wealth, of intimate family life, of comfort constantly renewed.
>
> — Henry James, *A New England Winter*

sending a young Harvard student, of the Class of 1887, on art-buying expeditions throughout Europe. This protégé was **Bernard Berenson** (1865–1959), who became an internationally known art historian and critic and *the* connoisseur of Renaissance art. His many books and monographs on Renaissance art and art appreciation were written with grace, knowledge, and style.

Ellis Grey Loring, "Beacon Street"

One of the scandalous aspects of Mrs. Jack's life was her wealth of male admirers, who buzzed about when her husband was alive. Though most scholars doubt that these liaisons were ever consummated, her relationship with the popular author **F. Marion Crawford** (1854–1909) may well have involved an affair. The son of Thomas Crawford, a sculptor, and a nephew of Julia Ward Howe, he published some four dozen popular romance novels, known for little more than their international settings and entertainment value.

Notice that the street numbers here skip from 150 to 154. That gap was created at the pleasure of Mrs. Gardner, who mandated that "her" 152 never be used on Beacon Street once she had moved.

Continue on Beacon to Exeter Street. Before turning left onto Exeter, look halfway down the right-hand side of the Exeter-Fairfield block. Here, at 296 Beacon, **Oliver Wendell Holmes**

spent the last twenty-three years of his life. Though born in Cambridge near Harvard Square and a resident of Charles Street for many years, in 1871 he moved to Beacon Street, where he entertained both people of medicine and people of letters.

Three doors down is 302 Beacon, yet another residence of the *Atlantic Monthly* editor **William Dean Howells** — a gentleman we've met in Louisburg Square and will meet again at the house he built in Cambridge.

Turning up Exeter, you'll come to Marlborough Street. About halfway down the street on your right is 239 Marlborough, where Robert Lowell moved with his second wife, the critic and novelist Elizabeth Hardwick, in 1955. **Robert Lowell, Jr.** (1917–1977), found life in the twentieth century — and life as a

Robert Lowell

member of the venerable Lowell clan — an uncomfortable fit. A rebel by nature, he transferred from Harvard to Kenyon College, converted to Catholicism, and became a conscientious objector during World War II. After spending several months in jail as a result, he published *Land of Unlikeness*, which won the Pulitzer Prize when it was expanded into *Lord Weary's Castle* (1945).

In the early and middle 1950s Lowell foundered, regaining his vision and direction partly with the help of contemporaries like Allen Ginsberg and William Carlos Williams and partly through psychiatric care at McLean Hospital in Belmont, Massachusetts. By the end of the decade, he was teaching at Boston University — where his

students included Sylvia Plath and Anne Sexton — and publishing his masterwork, *Life Studies* (1959). Both it and his powerful *For the Union Dead* (1964) placed Lowell at the head of the new breed of confessional poets in America.

Between 1949 and 1972, Lowell was married to **Elizabeth Hardwick** (b. 1916), the second of his three wives. Born in Kentucky, Hardwick, like her husband, was disenchanted with Boston in the 1950s. In her essay "Boston: The Lost Ideal" (1959), she mused on her theory that the city's period of intellectual superiority was long gone: *Boston — wrinkled, spindly-legged, depleted of nearly all her spiritual and cutaneous oils, provincial, self-esteeming — has gone on spending her inflated bills of pure reputation decade after decade. Now, one supposes, it is over at last.*

Hardwick and Lowell subsequently moved themselves to New York City. In her essay "The Genius of Margaret Fuller" (1986), Hardwick saw this escape route — savoring what little Boston had to offer, then moving on to Manhattan — similar to that of the brilliant Fuller more than a century before: *[Margaret Fuller] was born in the wrong place, the place thought to be the only right one for an American intellectual in the nineteenth century. That is, she was born in Cambridgeport, Massachusetts, around Harvard, Boston, Concord, and all the rest. She sprang out of the head of all the Zeuses about: her father Timothy Fuller, Emerson, Goethe. . . . [W]hat the whole span of her life shows is that she got all from being around Boston at the transfiguring moment, and would have lost all had she not escaped.*

Where Exeter crosses Commonwealth Avenue, you will see two significant men of action and letters seated on the left and the right of the Mall.

On the left you see the back of the abolitionist **William Lloyd Garrison** (1805–1879). Dedicated in 1886, this bronze statue by Olin Levi Warner was the first seated memorial on the Mall. Abandoned by a seafaring father, then raised by a poor deacon in Newburyport, Massachusetts, Garrison learned

William Lloyd Garrison, Commonwealth Avenue Mall

the newspaper trade as a youth. As editor of the *Free Press*, he was the first to publish the poems of John Greenleaf Whittier. Once committed to abolitionism, Garrison risked his life and livelihood by founding the New England Anti-Slavery Society and the American Anti-Slavery Society and publishing his unapologetic and outspoken newspaper, *The Liberator.*

Though many of his peers preferred to fight slavery with an entourage of white males, Garrison believed that women and African Americans were as important to the cause — and to his newspaper — as any privileged Brahmin. Garrison's wise face looks worn in Warner's bronze, but his hand grasps a bundle of papers with strength and conviction. It's a tribute to his progressive thinking that a man who was chased by a lynch mob through the streets of Boston in 1835 would be memorialized there only half a century later.

The seated sculpture facing you from the Exeter-Fairfield block is the maritime historian, **Samuel Eliot Morison** (1887–1976), whom we met at his childhood home near Charles Street. The piece, created by Penelope Jencks, was added to the Mall in 1982. Perched on a twenty-ton granite boulder, the native Bostonian and U.S. Navy admiral was a sailor, Harvard professor, a prolific author, and a Pulitzer Prize winner. Among his

> I am in earnest — I will not equivocate — I will not excuse — I will not retreat a single inch; and I will be heard!
>
> — William Lloyd Garrison, *The Liberator* (1831)

best-known books are *Builders of the Bay Colony* (1930), *The Founding of Harvard College* (1935), *The Growth of the American Republic* (1930, with Henry Steele Commager), and *The Oxford History of the American People* (1965). His Pulitzer Prizes were awarded for biographies of Christopher Columbus, *Admiral of the Ocean Sea* (1942), and *John Paul Jones* (1959).

One block farther, on the Fairfield-Gloucester stretch of the Mall, a new women's memorial is planned — the first sculpture on the Mall to celebrate women's accomplishments. It will depict the Revolutionary scribe Abigail Adams, the poet Phillis Wheatley, and the suffragist publisher Lucy Stone.

Before leaving Commonwealth Avenue, it is good to recall Edward Bellamy's (1850–1898) *Looking Backward: 2000–1887* (1888), in which Julian West falls into a hypnotic sleep in 1887 and awakens in a Commonwealth Avenue home in the year 2000. Influenced by nine-teenth-century utopianism, Bellamy idealized the Boston of the future as a socialist society, void of banks, lawyers, jails, crime, corruption, advertising, private enterprise, warfare, poverty, and all the other trappings of wayward American capitalism. In the new world order of social and economic justice that Julian West finds in 2000, culture, ethics, and intelligence are in abundance.

Plus ça change . . .

There are a handful of sites within several long blocks of the Literary Trail that are worth a side trip, together or individually:

If you continue down Beacon Street past Massachusetts Avenue and beyond the Charlesgate interchange, you will find Bay State

Samuel Eliot Morison, Commonwealth Avenue Mall

Road. During the last two years of his life, **Eugene O'Neill** (1888– 1953) and his wife, Carlotta (1888– 1970), lived at 91 Bay State Road. The winner of three Pulitzers and one Nobel Prize, O'Neill was a giant of twentieth-century American theater. His dozens of internationally acclaimed plays include *Beyond the Horizon* (1920), *Anna Christie* (1921), *Desire Under the Elms* (1924), *Strange Interlude* (1928), *Mourning Becomes Electra* (1931), *The Iceman Cometh* (1946), and *Long Day's Journey into Night* (written 1941, posthumously published 1956).

Eugene and Carlotta O'Neill

After studying playwriting in George Pierce Baker's 47 Workshop at Harvard, O'Neill founded the Provincetown Players, which first produced his work in 1916 on a rustic Cape Cod wharf. He soon gained the attention of the New York theater community, and a prolific period of writing followed. More than a decade later, O'Neill enjoyed the dubious honor of being "banned in Boston." In 1928, his long and experimental *Strange Interlude* was not allowed to play on Boston stages — though it proved a sellout in nearby Quincy. According to legend, many theatergoers took their intermission break at a fast-food operation run by local entrepreneur Howard Johnson, thereby boosting his business into profit and prominence.

Over his lifetime, O'Neill lived in a variety of places, including New York, France, and Marblehead, Massachusetts. During his last years he suffered from a progressive tremor and Parkinson's disease, making writing almost impossible. To be near his doctors in Boston, the O'Neills lived in Suite 401 in the Hotel Shelton, now a Boston University dormitory.

It was a great mistake, my being born a man, I would have been much more successful as a sea gull or a fish.

— Eugene O'Neill, *Long Day's Journey into Night* (1941)

If you continue down Commonwealth Avenue past Gloucester Street, you'll come to the last of the alphabet streets in the grid, Hereford. On the left, 40 Hereford was the home of "the Mother of Level Measurements," the internationally adored author of *The Boston Cooking-School Cook Book*, **Fannie Farmer** (1857–1915).

Born in Boston and raised in nearby Medford, Fannie Merritt Farmer began her cooking career in part because of a disability. Partially paralyzed at seventeen by either a stroke or a polio-like illness, she found herself unable to attend school or socialize. Confined to her home, she found solace and excitement in cooking, first for her family, and later for the boarders the Farmers took in. By the age of thirty, Farmer's culinary talents were so obvious that she was en-couraged to enter the reputable Boston Cooking School, at 174 Tremont Street. In the next four years, the graduate became assistant principal, then principal, of the school.

Next, of course, came the book. First published in 1896, the *Boston Cooking-School Cook Book* came to be known worldwide as simply *Fannie Farmer*. When Farmer first took the manuscript to Little, Brown, however, the prestigious house was dubious about its merits. When it turned her down, she agreed to pay for the printing of the first 3,000 copies personally. A century and well over three million copies later, the book, thoroughly revised, is still a staple of kitchens everywhere.

Farmer's crusade to take the old school of measuring — with a "heaping cup" here and a "rounded teaspoon" there — and bring it into the world of science was revolutionary in the annals of cooking. In this first edition of her book, she warned readers: *Correct measurements are absolutely necessary to insure the best results. . . . Good judgment, with experience, has taught some to measure by sight; but the majority need definite guides.*

In 1902, Farmer opened her own establishment, Miss Farmer's School of Cookery, at 30 Huntington Avenue. For a decade beginning in 1905, she also wrote monthly food columns in the *Woman's Home Companion*. Its

Fannie Farmer

editors were worried about upsetting her dedicated audience when she died, on January 15, 1915. As a result, they continued to run her columns until the end of the year, never mentioning her death.

Proceed to Massachusetts Avenue and turn left to the stoplight on Boylston Street. One block on the right, at 1154 Boylston, is the **Massachusetts Historical Society**.

Founded in 1791, the Historical Society first stored its collections of "curiosities" in temporary quarters that included the attic of Faneuil Hall. From 1833 to 1897, it occupied a building at 30 Tremont Street, next to the King's Chapel Burying Ground. It was here that Henry Wadsworth Longfellow read Paul Revere's own manuscript of his famous journey — inspiring him to write "Paul Revere's Ride." Published in 1863, in the midst of the Civil War, that poem became a "call to arms," linking one patriotic American war to another.

In 1899, the Historical Society moved to its present home. Though it maintains a modern research library, it continues to collect items that mark where history and literature intersect. Among those acquisitions are the papers of Ellery Sedgwick, editor of the *Atlantic Monthly* from 1908 to 1938. His correspondents ranged from Carl Sandburg and Virginia Woolf to Felix Frankfurter (on the Sacco and Vanzetti case) and

Robert Frost — who was initially rejected by the magazine. The society is a famed repository for the letters and diaries of historical figures from Governor John Winthrop to presidents John and John Quincy Adams. It also holds the papers of the romantic historians George Bancroft, William Hickling Prescott, and Francis Parkman. Henry Adams left his personal papers and library to the society, including the copyright to *The Education of Henry Adams*.

Just beyond the society, where Boylston meets the Fenway, is a bust of the distinguished Irish-American editor, orator, poet, and crusader for human rights, **John Boyle O'Reilly** (1844–1890). Sculpted by Daniel Chester French in 1896, the memorial commemorates the editor and co-owner of the powerful Irish-American Catholic newspaper *The Pilot*. A significant link between the new Irish immigrants and Boston's old Brahmin culture, O'Reilly was the poet of choice on a variety of historic occasions, including the reunion of the Army of the Potomac and the dedication of Plymouth Rock.

Return to the main route of the Literary Trail at the intersection of Commonwealth Avenue and Exeter Street. Continue on Exeter to Boylston Street — the closest thing modern Boston has to a Main

Street. A left on Boylston takes you into Copley Square, which holds two of Boston's architectural masterpieces: Trinity Church and the McKim Building of the Boston Public Library.

For centuries, libraries were the private domains of the learned, moneyed few. Even by the middle of the nineteenth century, the area's two largest book repositories were the private Boston Athenaeum and the Harvard College Library, accessible only to faculty and students. By 1854, however, literacy became the right of Everyman when the **Boston Public Library** opened its doors on Mason Street, near the Common, to become the country's first major free municipal library. The mass of immigrants who lived in the city by midcentury — and the Yankees' desire to educate and acculturate them — was a major incentive for creating both public libraries and public schools.

By 1895, the Boston Public Library had found a third, permanent home in Copley Square in a stunning structure designed by Charles Follen McKim and inspired by the Italian Renaissance. Entering the building from Dartmouth Street, you'll immediately notice three huge bronze doors in the vestibule, depicting Music and Poetry, Knowledge and Wisdom, and Truth and Romance, designed by Daniel Chester French. Some of the finest artists of the time — including French, Louis and Augustus Saint-Gaudens, John Singer Sargent, Puvis de Chavannes, and Edwin Austin Abbey — were called on to create decorative pieces for the library, both inside and out.

Once inside, you'll be in an ornate lobby of Roman design. Embedded in the mosaic domes above are the names of famous Bostonians, grouped into categories such as theologians, artists, reformers, and historians. The literary figures so commemorated include Hawthorne, Emerson, Longfellow, but — a testament to the times — not a single female. Ascend the main staircase, which Henry James loved for "its amplitude of wing and its splendour of tawny

The Grand Staircase, Boston Public Library

marble, a high and luxurious beauty."

At the top of the staircase is the building's centerpiece, the majestic, 218-foot-long Bates Hall. It was named for the wealthy financier Joshua Bates — a senior partner in Baring Brothers, the London banking firm — who had long dreamed of creating a grand reading room that would be open to the public without charge. As a poor boy growing up on the South Shore, Bates taught himself to read in the back rooms of Boston's bookstores. Bates's donation of $100,000 as well as some 30,000 books made him a major benefactor of the new library building.

On its opening, Bates Hall was compared to "the hall of a great Roman bath, with decorative elements of the Italian Renaissance superimposed." The reviewer for the *Boston Daily Globe* found himself almost speechless in his report of February 1, 1895: *Boston's new public library is done. It is the finest library building in the world, and contains the second largest collection of books and pamphlets in the United States. . . . Bates Hall is the apartment that has baffled all descriptive writers. It is so grand, so immense, and so noble in conception and effect, that it is beyond the limitation of words.*

One of the dreams behind the creation of public libraries — to serve and integrate the immigrant

> All persons using the Library must conduct themselves in such a manner as not to interfere with or cause annoyance to others; and to this end all annoying and disagreeable behavior, such as hawking, spitting on the floor, humming, whistling, whispering is strictly prohibited.
>
> — Rules and Regulations of the Public Library of the City of Boston, revised March 1896

population — was certainly fulfilled in Boston. A fine example is **Mary Antin** (1881–1949), who fled from Russian Poland's czarist regime in 1894 and came to the United States. Antin took every opportunity she could to improve her mind and her life in the land of the free. She attended public school in Boston, published poems in local newspapers as a child, and wrote *From Plotzk to Boston* — a chronicle of life in the Jewish Pale and her family's emigration — while still a youth. Among her many admirers was Edward Everett Hale, who gave her free run of his personal book collection.

In her autobiography, *The Promised Land* (1912), Antin applauded that other masterful book collection — the Boston

Public Library — as "a noble treasure house of learning": Public Library — Built by the People — Free to All. *Did I not say it was my palace? Mine, because I was a citizen; mine, though I was born an alien; mine, though I lived on Dover Street. My palace — mine!*

The library was just as beloved by great writers and scholars as by ordinary folk. The Alcott family, Ralph Waldo Emerson, Oliver Wendell Holmes, John Greenleaf Whittier, Lucy Larcom, Henry Wadsworth Longfellow, Sarah Orne Jewett, John Boyle O'Reilly, and Nathaniel Hawthorne were among those who worked here.

Today, the Boston Public Library remains a treasured gem, serving all the citizens of Massachusetts. It is one of only two public libraries qualified to belong to the Association of Research Libraries. The McKim Building has been declared a National Historic Landmark. Regular guided tours offer visitors an informed view of the institution, past and present,

Kahlil Gibran, circa 1910

including its wealth of fine art and architecture.

While in Copley Square, stop at the **Kahlil Gibran Monument**, across the street and directly facing the McKim Building.

Kahlil Gibran (1883–1931) was a first-generation Lebanese immigrant who lived and worked on Tyler Street, in Boston's Chinatown, where he wrote his most famous book, *The Prophet* (1923). A poet, philosopher, and artist, he was considered the genius of his age by Arabic-speaking people and has remained a source of spiritual insight and inspiration to all nationalities since his death. This

> You pray in your distress and in your need; would that you might pray also in the fullness of your joy and in your days of abundance.
>
> — Kahlil Gibran,
> *The Prophet* (1923)

memorial, a bronze bas-relief of the young poet on a pink granite slab, was sculpted by Kahlil Gibran, his godson, cousin, co-biographer, and namesake. It is inscribed with the poet's acknowledgment of the aid given him by Boston and its Brahmins: "It was in my heart to help a little because I was helped much." When the poet died, his body lay in a receiving tomb at Forest Hills Cemetery, in the Jamaica Plain neighborhood of Boston, before being shipped to Lebanon for interment.

OFF THE BEATEN PATH

Forest Hills Cemetery

APPROXIMATE TIME: 1–3 HOURS

Directions: Forest Hills Cemetery is located at 95 Forest Hills Avenue in Jamaica Plain. From Park Drive or Brookline Avenue, take the winding Jamaicaway to the Arnold Arboretum. Continue around the rotary onto Route 203 East, past the Arboretum's main entrance, then go one more mile, crossing the Casey overpass, to the Forest Hills rotary. The entrance to the cemetery is just beyond, at the junction of Morton Street (203 E) and Forest Hills Avenue. By public transportation, the cemetery is a short walk from the Forest Hills MBTA stop, on the Orange Line.

The Puritans who settled New England warned of fiery post-mortem death in their sermons and disposed of their dead accordingly. Colonial Boston's graveyards became bleak repositories that reflected the harsh realities of life and a hellfire-and-damnation view of death. Gravestones were often stark slate markers, simply carved with names and dates or decorated with symbols like a skull and crossbones, the Grim Reaper, an hourglass, or a death's head. Gravesites were used again and again, with family, friends, and strangers piling one upon another, sometimes five and six deep.

By the early nineteenth century, these burying grounds were often overcrowded with bodies, overgrown with weeds, and generally decrepit. They were also assumed to be the source of noxious odors and contagious disease. However, new, romantic attitudes about death and the afterlife had come into fashion by this time. Rather than focusing on eternal damnation like their colonial ancestors, many began to see death as an ethereal repose. Writers such as John Milton and Alexander Pope observed that properly "shaped" land was capable of evoking nostalgia and profound emotion. Hence, burying grounds that were more attuned to nature, more conducive to calm and eternal rest, began to emerge. Following the model of English pleasure parks and Père Lachaise Cemetery in Paris, Americans embarked on a new era of burial practice. The church graveyard gave way to the "cemetery," a term culled from the French *cimitière*, a place of rest.

In 1831, the first rural garden cemetery in America, Mount Auburn, was dedicated in Cambridge, Massachusetts. Seventeen years later, Forest Hills —in historic Roxbury, now the Jamaica Plain neighborhood of Boston — was consecrated as a city cemetery. Though Mount Auburn was private and Forest Hills originally municipal (it became private after two decades), they shared a similar design and vision: beautifully carved memorials, often by famous sculptors, were scattered over naturally landscaped hills and dales, laced with winding paths, wistful trees and plantings, and reflective pools of water. Poignant, often literary, inscriptions were carved on their intricately designed stones. Both cemeteries, as a result, attracted creative, nature-loving people who wished to spend eternity in a quiet and artful rural setting.

At the main gate of Forest Hills, pick up a large street map to guide you through the 280-acre cemetery and help you find individual memorials. Also, a comprehensive book and self-guided walking tour, *Garden of Memories: A Guide to Historic Forest Hills*, can be purchased at the front office.

Though people from all social classes, races, religions, and professions have been buried here, there are a great number of authors, playwrights, poets, journalists, and historians, including many of those on the Literary Trail: the playwright Eugene O'Neill, the poets e. e. cummings and Anne Sexton, the writers Edward Everett Hale, Susanna Haswell Rowson, and George Ticknor, and the abolitonists William Lloyd Garrison and William Cooper Nell.

Daniel Chester French is also present in the form of some of his finest work. Directly beyond the main gate, you can see his funerary masterpiece, *Death and the Sculptor*, a high-relief bronze tribute to his fellow artists Martin and Joseph Milmore. Curiously, the sculptor depicted in this work is carving a Sphinx, thus referring directly to the Civil War memorial that Martin Milmore created for Mount Auburn Cemetery and that faces Bigelow Chapel to this day. French has several other pieces at Forest Hills, including a winged tribute to one of Boston's major benefactors, George Robert White (who is also memorialized by a statue in the Public Garden). Meanwhile, Forest Hills

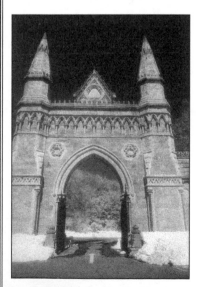

Forest Hills Cemetery entrance

remains highly regarded for its wealth of Victorian memorial sculpture — arguably the finest collection in the nation.

A variety of literary figures not yet encountered on the Literary Trail are also interred at Forest Hills. Among them are the writers Nancy Hale Bowers (*The Young Die Good*) and Frederick Lewis Allen (*Only Yesterday*), the historians Annie Haven Thwing (*The Crooked and Narrow Streets of Boston*) and Samuel Gardner Drake (*Indian Biographies*), the diarist Anna Cabot Lowell (*Journal of My Conduct*), and the composer Amy Marcy Cheney Beach, the first American woman to write a symphony.

Charles H. Taylor, the first member of the *Boston Globe* dynasty, is buried here, as is the radical German-American editor Karl Heinzen (*Pionier*). John Sullivan Dwight, the acclaimed nineteenth-century music critic and literary reviewer, and Curtis Guild, Sr., the writer, drama critic, and newspaperman who founded Boston's *Commercial Bulletin*, one of the most important business journals of its day, can also be found here. Clarence Walker Barron, the father of modern financial analysis and an owner of the *Wall Street Journal*, is interred here as well. *Barron's* magazine still bears his name.

Herbert Mosely Plimpton, a bookbinder, is also a resident of Forest Hills. He was the founder of the Plimpton Press, the largest book bindery in New England. It helped pioneer the process of moving a book through the complete process, from manuscript to bound volume, in a single plant.

Among the many interesting tales in the annals of Forest Hills are these two, concerning Eugene O'Neill and e. e. cummings:

When O'Neill died in the Hotel Shelton on November 27, 1953, he had already created his obituary notice: "Born in a goddam hotel room and dying in a hotel room!" To avoid the public and the press, his wife had J. S. Waterman & Sons Funeral Home quietly whisk her husband away to Forest Hills — no fanfare, flash bulbs, or elaborate funeral. Though fans stole flowers and other tokens from the gravesite for years thereafter, today they tend to leave gifts instead: a small cairn, or memorial rock pile, is often found on O'Neill's headstone.

After cummings died of a cerebral hemorrhage on September 3, 1962, he was buried in Forest Hills in the lot of the Clarkes — his mother's side of the family. Ironically, the man known for his calculated disregard for uppercase letters was memorialized with a simple flush marker that reads EDWARD ESTLIN CUMMINGS in bold capitals. One of his most telling observations on death can be found in his poem "Since Feeling Is First":

> *for life's not*
> *a paragraph and*
> *death I think*
> *is no parenthesis.*

The Literary Trail now moves on to Cambridge. If you are leaving the Boston Public Library by car, head west on the Massachusetts Turnpike from Copley Square.

Driving on the Mass. Pike, you'll soon see the floodlights of Fenway Park hovering on your left. Fabulous Fenway — the home of the Boston Red Sox since 1912 — has inspired countless literary musings. Among the classics is John Updike's "Hub Fans Bid Kid Adieu," written after seeing Ted Williams play his last game on September 28, 1960: *Our noise for some seconds passed beyond excitement into a kind of immense open anguish, a cry to be saved. But immortality is not transferable. The papers said that the other players, and even the umpires on the field, begged him to come out and acknowledge us in some way, but he never had and did not now. Gods do not answer letters.*

In 1999 the master of the macabre, **Stephen King** (b. 1947), used a Red Sox relief hitter as the inspiration for his best-selling novel *The Girl Who Loved Tom Gordon.* The popular writer has also been a prolific one, writing new horror and science fiction novels almost every year for some time.

Leave the Mass. Pike at the Cambridge/Allston exit, staying to the right. Continue straight over the bridge across the Charles River. The river, of course, has inspired many writers throughout Boston's history, including Annie Adams Fields: *[Before the embankments were added, the Charles River] was wider and more beautiful. Early in the morning, sometimes before sunrise, standing at my bedroom window I have seen [Oliver Wendell Holmes's] tiny skiff moving quickly over the face of the quiet water. Sometimes the waves were high and rough. . . . There was little to be learned about a skiff and its management which he did not acquire.*

Once over the Charles, take a left onto Memorial Drive. The well-maintained Riverside Press Park, immediately on your right, is the site of the **Riverside Press**, an important chapter in Boston's publishing history. In 1846, a twenty-three-year-old Vermonter named Henry O. Houghton moved to Cambridge and set up his printing shop near Harvard. When his business outgrew the modest space, he moved his firm to the banks of the Charles — to a building on River Street that had been built as an

> I have just returned from Boston. It is the only sane thing to do if you find yourself up there.
>
> — Fred Allen, *Letter to Groucho Marx* (1953)

almshouse for the city in 1838. Little, Brown & Company had purchased the building earlier that year and converted it to a printing plant.

Houghton's Riverside Press served many prestigious publishing houses such as Little, Brown, G. C. Merriam, and Ticknor & Fields — also printing the latter's popular magazine, the *Atlantic Monthly*. Meanwhile, as William Ticknor and James T. Fields and their Old Corner Bookstore grew, so too did Henry Houghton and his printing plant. Fields became the sole proprietor of his firm after Ticknor's death in 1864. Houghton took on George Harrison Mifflin as a partner in 1872.

By 1880, the Boston publisher and Cambridge printer merged, creating Houghton, Mifflin & Company. The Riverside Press was maintained as a subsidiary until 1966 and the Ticknor & Fields imprint restored as a tribute to the old company from 1979 to 1992. The facility on this site was closed by Houghton Mifflin in 1971 and the building was demolished two years later. A coalition of city and neighborhood workers created and dedicated the namesake Riverside Press Park in 1981.

Follow Memorial Drive, with the river on your left, until you turn right into Harvard Square on John F. Kennedy Street. Driving

> Boston has opened and kept open, more turnpikes that lead straight to free thought and free speech and free deeds than any other city of live or dead men.
>
> — Oliver Wendell Holmes

toward the Square, you'll pass Harvard's John F. Kennedy Park and the John F. Kennedy School of Government on your left. Countless great names in government, politics, public affairs, and history have taught, lectured, attended classes, or otherwise passed through its doors, including Marvin Kalb (*Kissinger*), Graham Allison (*Essence of Decision*), and Richard Neustadt and Ernest May (*The Uses of History*).

Glance to the left as you pass Eliot Street. Behind the Kennedy School you can see the elegant Charles Hotel complex, which includes a fitness center frequented by **Robert B. Parker** (b. 1932). Like his fictional gumshoe, the man known simply as Spenser, Parker is famous for keeping in shape. The very literate and likable Spenser, meanwhile, has appeared in more than two dozen novels. His character has also been spun off into a popular 1980s TV series (*Spenser for Hire*) and a new run of movies for cable TV.

Cambridge

THE HISTORIES OF BOSTON and Cambridge have so intertwined over the centuries that many people assume they are two parts of a single city. Cambridge was actually founded in 1630 as Newtowne by the same English colonists who had settled Boston a few months earlier. Both towns played major roles in the crises, cries, and conflicts that resulted in the American Revolution by 1775. And both have proved pivotal in the development of American literary and cultural life from colonial times through the present day.

When Harvard College was founded in 1636 — the first institution of higher learning in Britain's North American colonies — it established Cambridge as an intellectual center. As a result, Cambridge boasted the first printing press in the colonies (1638) and swiftly became a magnet for writers, educators, and academicians. By the nineteenth and twentieth centuries, this group included many of the leading literary figures in the country, from Henry James, Alice James, Henry Wadsworth Longfellow, Margaret Fuller, Robert Frost, and Eugene O'Neill to e. e. cummings, Gertrude Stein, Vladimir Nabokov, May Sarton, Helen Vendler, Cornel West, and Henry Louis Gates, Jr.

William Dean Howells, himself a writer and editor, made note of the extraordinary bounty in *Literary Friends and Acquaintances* (1900): *The variety of talents and achievements was indeed so great that Mr. Bret Harte . . . justly said . . . "Why, you couldn't fire a revolver from your front porch anywhere [in Cambridge] without bringing down a two-volumer!"* The reclusive poet Emily Dickinson reacted to this phenomenon with awe and appreciation: *[Moving to Cambridge is] like moving to Westminster Abbey, as hallowed and as unbelieved, or moving to Ephesus with Paul for a next-door neighbor.*

The two areas of Cambridge (map, p. 94) most closely associated with the Golden Age of American Literature are the **Harvard University** campus — flowing in and out of Harvard Yard and Harvard Square — and **Brattle Street.**

After following John F. Kennedy

> Youth is the time of getting, middle age of improving, and old age of spending.
>
> —Anne Bradstreet,
> *Meditations Divine and Moral* (1664)

Street from the Charles River to Harvard Square, pause at the center of the Square. To the right is a pedestrian mall, where you'll see an entrance to the "T," a Bostix ticket booth, and the famed Out of Town newsstand. In 1631, **Anne Bradstreet** (ca. 1612–1672), the colonies' first female poet, made her home on this site, facing today's Harvard Yard.

The daughter of Thomas Dudley, an early governor of the Massachusetts Bay Colony, Anne married Simon Bradstreet at the age of sixteen and arrived in America on the ship *Arbella* in 1630. In the early days of the Puritan settlement, literature rarely strayed from religious sermons and personal journals. Despite the restrictive atmosphere — and the time and energy it took to raise eight children while supporting her hus-

band's political ambitions — Anne wrote poems, prose "meditations," and letters, publishing more than four hundred pages of verse during her lifetime.

Though some consider her poetry unoriginal, Shaun O'Connell noted in *Imagining Boston* that "Bradstreet's spiritual autobiography helped define a literary mode which would persist, with telling variations and revisions, for three centuries." In 1964, the poet **John Berryman** (1914–1972) wrote the lengthy *Homage to Mistress Bradstreet,* who proved an inspiration to him three centuries after her death. Berryman, like Bradstreet, once lived in Harvard Square. Today, Harvard's Houghton Library, on the opposite side of Harvard Yard from the spot where the poet lived, maintains Bradstreet's original manuscripts.

> It is a true error to marry
>   with poets
> or to be by them.
>
> — John Berryman,
>   *77 Dream Songs* (1964)

Harvard Square

APPROXIMATE TIME: 90 MINUTES

Harvard Square, often called simply "the Square," was named for its proximity to the Harvard College campus. Though there are other bustling, commercial "squares" in Cambridge — notably Central, Kendall, Inman, and Porter — Harvard Square has asserted its dominance in things cultural for close to four centuries.

Begin this walking trip at the site of the poet Anne Bradstreet's home, near the Out of Town newsstand. As you walk up Mass. Ave. past the Cambridge Savings Bank, you'll see Dunster Street, parallel to JFK Street, on your right. Around the corner of Dunster and up one story on the brick façade is a plaque honoring Stephen Day, who lived on this site. Day established **America's first printing press** nearby in 1638 and ran it under the auspices of the infant college. Among his early printing projects was the *Bay Psalm Book,* the colonies' first collection of metrical versions of the psalms; it became the most popular English psalter. Though seventeen hundred copies of the book were printed in 1640, fewer than a

dozen survive. The *Bay Psalm Book* had three prestigious editors: the Reverend Richard Mather, the first of the line of Mathers to settle in the New World; the Reverend John Eliot, the famed "Apostle to the Indians"; and the Reverend Thomas Weld, an ancestor of the governor of Massachusetts some three and a half centuries later. (William Weld is an author himself. After leaving office in 1997, he turned to writing mysteries, beginning with *Mackerel by Moonlight.*)

One block farther, the corner of Mass. Ave. and Holyoke Street once held the University Book Store, run by the prodigious reader and entrepreneur **John Bartlett** (1820–1905). Famous for his ability to recall the sources of quotations, Bartlett published his first volume of *Familiar Quotations* in 1855.

Because of its extensive literary history, academic appeal, and large student population, the city has always had a wide and diverse array of bookshops. Cambridge actually boasts more bookstores per capita than any city in the world — some thirty-six in all, twenty-four of which are in Harvard Square. The **Out of Town Newsstand** at the center of Harvard Square stocks newspapers and journals from around the world.

Two blocks beyond Holyoke Street on Mass. Ave. is Plympton Steet. The venerable **Grolier Poetry Book Shop,** at 6 Plympton, has been an important gathering and performance space for

---

AUTHOR / AUTHOR!

Justin Kaplan on John Bartlett and his *Familiar Quotations*

One of the books I brought with me when I came to Harvard as a freshman in 1941 was an edition of *Bartlett's Familiar Quotations*. I hadn't realized then that my room at Apley Court was just around the corner from the site of the bookstore Bartlett owned before the Civil War, that he lived on Brattle Street, a short distance from his friends Henry Wadsworth Longfellow and James Russell Lowell, and that he's buried in nearby Mount Auburn Cemetery, the nation's first and probably most beautiful "park of repose." Many decades later I was privileged to succeed (in a limited sense) Bartlett as editor of *Familiar Quotations*. Over the century and a half since its first edition came out this wonderful old warhorse of a reference book has been regularly updated and enlarged in order to shuck off the time-worn and irrelevant, take in the fresh and timely, and cast a wider net.

Born in 1820, John Bartlett lived to see his name become as generic for quotations as Noah Webster's for definitions. He read widely, kept notes on his reading, and made himself an information bank for members of the local history and academic community. They turned to Bartlett when they wanted to know who said what, when, and where. In 1855 he brought out his first collection of "phrases and familiar quotations which have become 'household words.'" By the time he died in 1905 he had brought out nine editions in all.

A remarkably energetic man, Bartlett had many interests other than quotations. He was an acknowledged authority on fishing, chess, and whist, and estimated he had spent sixteen thousand hours compiling, with the help of his wife Hannah, a concordance to Shakespeare.

writers and poets since 1927. The store has been revered and inhabited by four generations of poets and their friends, garnering such accolades as *Boston Magazine*'s Best-of-Boston Award ("Best Poetry Store and Readings") to this day.

Next door, 8 Plympton was once the home of **Conrad Aiken** (1889– 1973), a novelist, critic, anthologist, and Pulitzer Prize–winning poet. Aiken moved here in 1915 to be near his mentor, John Gould Fletcher. Meanwhile, in 1929, the British novelist **Malcolm Lowry** (1909–1957) came to work with Aiken as an apprentice.

Just beyond, number 14 is the home of the Harvard *Crimson*, the spawning ground of many great writers and journalists. **Richard Wilbur** (b. 1921), a prize-winning poet and translator, lived at 22 Plympton while working on his master's degree at Harvard after World War II. Like so many other graduates, Wilbur went on to teach at Harvard and other institutions.

The oddly shaped, colorful building where Plympton meets Bow Street, at 44 Bow, belongs to the *Harvard Lampoon.* Founded in 1876, it is the world's oldest continuously published humor magazine. An inordinate number of *Lampoon* alumni have become

Hollywood scriptwriters and include some of America's finest literary talent. John Updike, George Plimpton, William Gaddis, George Santayana, and the publisher William Randolph Hearst — who gave the magazine its building — were all 'Poonies. Robert Benchley, who edited the *Lampoon* with Frederick Lewis Allen (*Only Yesterday*) in the 1920s, made the ultimate observation about pens, popularity, and self-knowledge: *It took me fifteen years to discover that I had no talent for writing, but I couldn't give it up because by that time I was too famous.*

Standing by the *Lampoon*, look toward the river to see a tall white spire topped by an ornate weathervane dominating the skyline. This is Lowell House, one of Harvard's undergraduate residence halls, where the Pulitzer Prize–winner **John Updike**

John Updike

(b.1932) spent his college years. Known best for his novels *Rabbit Run, Rabbit Redux,* and *The Witches of Eastwick,* Updike has written more than forty books, including novels, short stories, poetry, and criticism, and is the only living author to have won the Pulitzer Prize for fiction twice. Well aware of the Boston area's literary heritage, he based one trilogy — *Roger's Version, A Month of Sundays,* and *S.* — on Hawthorne's *Scarlet Letter.* Updike chose Ipswich, on the North Shore, as his permanent home.

A stone's throw from the intersection of Plympton and Mount Auburn, at 47 Mount Auburn Street, was the original **Club 47**, as nurturing a space for the musicians of the Great Folk Revival of the 1960s as the Grolier was for poets. From 1958 to 1968, Club 47 was the stomping grounds of influential and internationally known folksingers, poets, and singer-songwriters like Joan Baez, Bob Dylan, Eric Von Schmidt, Tom Rush, Richard Fariña, Judy Collins, and the Charles River Valley Boys. By far the best book on the folk scene of the '60s is Eric Von Schmidt and Jim Rooney's *Baby Let Me Follow You Down: The Illustrated Story of the Cambridge Folk Years* (1979).

This performance venue — now called **Club Passim** and located at 47 Palmer Street, just off Church Street in Harvard Square — remains a haven for that literary-musical tradition to this day. The inimitable Bob Donlin, who ran Passim with his wife, Rae Anne, from 1969 through 1995, was one of Jack Kerouac's "dharma bums," loosely disguised as Bob Donnelly in Kerouac's novels. Meanwhile, the club has helped to introduce a whole new generation of talents, musical and literary, including Suzanne Vega, Shawn Colvin, Nanci Griffith, Bill Morrissey, Patty Larkin, and Tracy Chapman.

Return on Plympton to Mass. Ave. Cross the street, turning right on Mass. Ave., then left

The Houghton Library

onto Quincy Street. Entering Harvard Yard through the first gate on your left, you'll be walking directly toward the **Houghton Library,** which contains the manuscripts and rare books belonging to the Harvard College Library. Opened in 1942, Houghton is an international resource of exceptional depth and diversity, offering scholars direct access to a wealth of primary sources. The collections, which focus on the study of Western civilization, include the working papers of living novelists and poets as well as the personal effects, notes, books, and other objects of interest from writers such as Copernicus, Emily Dickinson, John Keats, Edward Lear, Dante, Tennessee Williams, Goethe, Cervantes, and Lewis Carroll.

Directly across the street from Houghton, in the Barker Center at 12 Quincy Street, is the **W.E.B. Du Bois Institute of Harvard University**, which is named for

W.E.B. Du Bois

William Edward Burghardt Du Bois, the first African American awarded a Ph.D. from Harvard (1895). Du Bois is often considered the most influential black thinker of the first half of the twentieth century. His many accomplishments range from numerous articles and books, including *The Souls of Black Folk* and *John Brown*, to helping to establish the National Association for the Advancement of Colored People (NAACP) in 1909. Du Bois lived several blocks away, on Flagg Street.

Continuing down Quincy Street, on the right you will see gateposts numbered 16 and 20.

Richard Henry Dana, Jr. (1815–1882), lived at 16 Quincy. Like so many youth of his era — who seemed to suffer unduly from ailments of the eyes and

> Believe in life! Always human beings will live and progress to greater, broader, and fuller life.
>
> — W.E.B. Du Bois, *Last Message to the World* (1963)

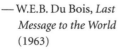

Henry Louis Gates, Jr. on W.E.B. Du Bois

William Edward Burghardt Du Bois was born in Great Barrington, Massachusetts, in 1869, and died in Accra, Ghana, on the eve of the great protest March on Washington in 1963. In his long life, which stretched from Reconstruction to the modern Civil Rights Movement, he became the leading African American public intellectual, the chief spokesperson for racial equality in America, and the symbol of world-wide Pan-Africanism. Du Bois's Greater Boston connections were strengthened by his study at Harvard University where he took a B.A. in 1890, and a Ph.D. in history in 1895, the first black American to do so. As an author, Du Bois wrote in every conceivable genre: essays, historical monographs, sociological studies, fiction, biographies, editiorials and news reports, and even three autobiographies. His *The Souls of Black Folk* (1903) is arguably the most important book written by an African American. He is probably best remembered for his prophetic prediction, "The problem of the twentieth century is the problem of the color line."

Du Bois particularly inspired and influenced me with his vision of an accurate and comprehensive encyclopedia on Africa and the lives and cultures of peoples of African descent throughout the world. It has been my privilege to co-edit with K. Anthony Appiah an encyclopedia on CD-ROM entitled *Encarta Africana* which, I believe, fulfills Du Bois's dream to correct historical inaccuracies, to cover materials ignored in standard reference works, and to see the African Diaspora whole. This is the deepest tribute I know how to pay to the memory of a great American fighter for justice, a literary figure of immense significance, and a New Englander of international stature.

nerves — Dana was the victim of failing eyesight. Abandoning his studies at Harvard in 1834, he signed up as a sailor on a brig bound for California. Invigorated by his adventures on the sea, as well as by a year working the hide-trading ports of California, Dana returned home with healed spirits and vision. The book for which he is still remembered, *Two Years Before the Mast* (1840), was the result of those travels.

Although the book was an immediate success and helped to win the passage of new laws for the protection of sailors, Dana never produced any volume that popular again. He graduated from Harvard Law School in 1839 and became a prime defender in the Anthony Burns fugitive slave trial. Thereafter, in his own judgment, he failed to live up to his youthful promise.

Where the Harvard Faculty Club now stands, at 20 Quincy, was once the James family home. Both **Henry James, Jr.** (1843–1916), and his brilliant, troubled sister, **Alice James** (1848–1892), lived here.

One of five offspring of his namesake father, Henry James had an eclectic education. Fascinated by theology, he attended Princeton Theological Seminary for two years and was long interested in the tenets of Swedenborgian thought. Though he lived and studied in New York, England, France, and Germany for extended periods, at the end of the Civil War, he finally settled in Boston at the age of twenty-one.

All of his travels and studies ultimately filtered into his adult world of literature and writing. After being "discovered" and befriended by William Dean Howells, James saw his first stories, essays, and criticisms printed in the *Atlantic Monthly.* His writings quickly impressed the New England *literati* as well as English masters like Tennyson and Ruskin. By 1869, James followed his reputation across the Atlantic, ultimately making his permanent home in England. Boston, in his opinion, was not a worthy place to live and work, being decidedly short on culture, aesthetics, and inspiration.

Over the next four decades James established himself as one of America's greatest novelists. Ironically, he also became one of the nation's best-known expatriates. He eventually became a British citizen, explaining, "I have testified

Henry James

to my long attachment here in the only way I could — though I certainly shouldn't have done it . . . if the U.S.A. had done a little more for me." George Bernard Shaw wryly observed that the move was a subtle one: "James felt buried in America; but he came here to be embalmed."

Though his topics and characters varied widely, James frequently wrote about the moral struggles of Americans in their homeland, the plight of Americans abroad, and the difficulties they had moving into European society. A sampling of his prodigious number of books, many of which have been made into movies, includes *The Europeans* (1878), *Hawthorne* (1879), *Daisy Miller* (1879), *Washington Square* (1881), *The Portrait of a Lady* (1881), *The Bostonians* (1886), and *The Wings of the Dove* (1902).

James was not afraid of strong women — nor of late-nineteenth-century feminism — like many of his literary peers. When female protagonists appeared in *Daisy Miller* and *Portrait of a Lady,* they were often in search of independence. Part of James's view of women came from his fascination with the "Boston marriage" of Sarah Orne Jewett and Annie Fields after the death of James T. Fields in 1881. His

acceptance of their partnership helped him understand and honor the same relationship his sister Alice had with Katharine Loring. These women, as well as the feminist Elizabeth Peabody, helped to inspire James's characters in *The Bostonians.*

Being the sister of Henry and William James was not easy for Alice James. Like William, she was often incapacitated by psychosomatic illnesses and severe depression. It wasn't until she met Loring, who cared for her as a semi-invalid, that the gifted and enigmatic Alice began to blossom. Her journals, which Henry considered beautiful, eloquent, and filled with independence, became beacons for later generations of feminists — including the poetry cooperative that formed Alice James Books in 1973. Originally published as her *Journal* (1894, 1934), Alice James's complete writings later appeared under the title *Diary*

> The moral is that the flower of art blooms only where the soil is deep, that it takes a great deal of history to produce a little literature, that it needs a complex machinery to set a writer in motion.
>
> — Henry James, *Hawthorne* (1879)

Memorial Hall

served or died in the Civil War, Memorial Hall was also built to house an academic theater for literary festivals and a dining hall large enough for Commencement dinners.

At its completion in 1878, Henry James found Memorial Hall a curiously ironic structure, "the great bristling brick Valhalla . . . that house of honor and hospitality which . . . dispenses . . . laurels to the dead and dinners to the living." A century later, Jane Langton found it a splendid site for a murder. In *The Memorial Hall Murder* (1978), Homer Kelly investigates the death of a chorus leader in the bowels of the building: *The building rose above him like a cliff face, mass piled upon mass, ten thousand of brick laid upon ten thousand. It was ugly, majestically ugly. Augustly, monumentally ugly. It was a red-brick Notre Dame, a bastard Chartres, punctured with stained-glass windows, ribboned around with lofty sentiments in Latin, finialed with metallic crests and pennants, knobbed with the heads of orators. . . . When it had been erected in the 1870s it had been intended as a half-secular, half-sacred memorial to young graduates who had died in the Union cause in the Civil War. Now it was an actual coffin.*

(1964). A fine study of her life is found in Jean Strouse's *Alice James: A Biography* (1980).

A sense of Alice James's unusual strength of spirit can be seen in this entry of November 19, 1889: *When will women begin to have the first glimmer that above all other loyalties is the loyalty to Truth, i.e. to yourself, that husbands, children, friends, and country are as nothing to that?*

Follow Quincy Street across Broadway and Cambridge Street. Dominating your view on the left is Harvard's Ruskinian Gothic structure known as **Memorial Hall**. Conceived as a living memorial to alumni who

The interior vestibule of Memorial Hall, which separates Sanders Theatre from the huge dining hall, is lined with lofty Latin inscriptions above twenty-eight white marble tablets naming the Civil War dead. In the 1984 film version of James's *Bostonians*, Christopher Reeve — as the southern Civil War veteran Basil Ransom — stands here, pondering these tablets. There was plenty to ponder: the 136 dead listed on the walls are Union men, while some 64 slain Confederate graduates are never mentioned.

Leaving Memorial Hall, bear right onto Kirkland Street and walk the several blocks to Francis Street. Follow Francis to its intersection with Bryant. Here on the left is the Harvard Divinity School campus.

Since its founding in 1636, Harvard College — immersed, as it was, in a Puritan stronghold — was closely tied to the Puritan church. Most of the men attending the school in its earliest decades studied religion, though not all went on to become preachers. And though Harvard was indeed expected to provide the British colonies with a learned clergy, the advancement of learning in general, for "the English and Indian Youth of this Country," was the school's broadest purpose, as outlined in its Charter of 1650.

Harvard Divinity School was founded in 1819 and emerged as a hotbed of Unitarianism. Among the many writers and ministers who studied here were William Ellery Channing, Horatio Alger, Jr., Frederic Dan Huntington, Thomas Wentworth Higginson, Ralph Waldo Emerson, Francis Greenwood Peabody, and the Reverend Peter J. Gomes.

One of the least divine was arguably **Horatio Alger, Jr.** (1832–1899). A native of Revere, Massachusetts, from an old Puritan family, Alger was primed for the ministry by his father, a Unitarian clergyman. Graduating from Harvard, he tended to his congregation in Brewster, Massachusetts. Unfortunately, Alger also tended to the choirboys in this small Cape Cod town and was run out of the church for his untoward behavior.

Alger soon found another career that, perhaps ironically, was also centered on boys. While still in Boston, Alger had agreed to create a boy's book with an uplifting message for the pub-lisher and bookseller A. K. Loring, at 319 Washington Street. The happy result was *Frank's Campaign, or What Boys Can Do on the Farm for the Camp*. Moving to New York, Alger became a chaplain and philanthropist for the Newsboys' Lodging House. There he began producing the stream of boys' books that brought him international fame.

The first of the truly successful Horatio Alger stories — tales in which poor boys struggled against adversity and temptation to find success, fame, and wealth — starred Ragged Dick. He was followed by Luck and Pluck, Tattered Tom, and sales in the millions. This phenomenal success led one critic to observe: "Horatio Alger wrote the same novel 135 times and never lost his audience."

On the corner of Bryant and Irving, at 136 Irving Street, is the rear entrance of the **American Academy of Arts and Sciences.** Founded in 1780 during the American Revolution, this scholarly society has always made its headquarters in the Boston area, although it does have other regional centers. In the first decades of the new republic, the members met in the Philosophy Chamber of Harvard College. After sharing quarters with the

Boston Athenaeum and later with the Massachusetts Historical Society for many years, the group found a twentieth-century home at 28 Newbury Street. In 1981 it moved to its own building in the beautifully wooded area that was once part of the Shady Hill estate of Charles Eliot Norton, a prominent nineteenth-century art historian at Harvard and editor of the *North American Review* and the *Nation*.

The American Academy's charter stated that its goal was "to cultivate every art and science which may tend to advance the interest, honour, dignity, and happiness of a free, independent and virtuous people." Today, it elects women and men of exceptional achievement to its ranks and conducts projects and studies "responsive to the needs and problems of society." The group also publishes the quarterly journal *Daedalus* and awards an Emerson-Thoreau medal for achievement in literature.

The roster of Academy fellows

over the past two centuries is a veritable *Who's Who* of important Americans in science, scholarship, business, public affairs, and the arts. Its literary members over the years include Henry Wadsworth Longfellow, Ralph Waldo Emerson, Daniel Webster, Henry Adams, Henry James, Oliver Wendell Holmes, Samuel Eliot Morison, Willa Cather, May Sarton, and Robert Pinsky.

Though originally limited to men, the Academy welcomed the astronomer and educator Maria Mitchell (1818–1889) to its membership in 1848. Today, some 17% of its 3,600 fellows and 600 Foreign Honorary Members are women. For almost a century, Mitchell was the sole female thus honored.

Follow Irving Street down to Scott and Farrar. Behind the Irving-Scott signpost is a historic marker noting that **e. e. cummings** (1894–1962) was born here, at 104A Irving. The sign also reminds visitors of one of his most quoted lines, from *Sonnets — Realities* (1923):

*the Cambridge ladies who live in
    furnished souls
are unbeautiful and have comfort-
    able minds.*

The son of Rebecca Haswell and Dr. Edward Cummings, the

---

mr u will not be missed
who as an anthologist
sold the many on the few
not excluding mr u

   — e. e. cummings, *1 x 1*
   (1944)

successor to Edward Everett Hale at Boston's Second Congregational Church, the young Edward Estlin Cummings attended Cambridge Latin School and Harvard College (Class of 1915) before running off to join the French ambulance corps in World War I. An accidental imprisonment in a concentration camp gave him material for *The Enormous Room* (1922), his first widely acclaimed novel.

From there cummings leapt into America's second great literary renaissance, experimenting with a new, free style of prose and poetry and distinguishing himself as a painter and playwright. The poet became known for not using capital letters — a conceit he explained in several ways. A student of Latin and Greek at Harvard, he observed that classical literature "never began a sentence with a capital." Moreover, he noted, no other language he knew of wrote the first-person singular — the ubiquitous "I" — in capitals.

Throughout his life, cummings spent a considerable time in Paris, Greenwich Village, and his family's rural retreat at Joy Farm, in Silver Lake, New Hampshire. During 1952–1953 he was Charles Eliot Norton Professor of Poetry at Harvard, where he delivered his famous series of "non-lectures." In *i:six non-lectures* (1953), cummings beautifully described 104 Irving: *My own home faced the Cambridge world as a finely and solidly constructed mansion, preceded by a large oval lawn and ringed with an imposing white-pine hedge. Just in front of the house itself stood two huge appletrees; and faithfully, every spring, these giants lifted their worlds of fragrance toward the room where I breathed and dreamed. . . . One of the many wonderful things about a home is that it can be as lively as you please without ever becoming public. The big Cambridge house was in this respect, as in all other respects, a true home.*

On the white picket fence across the street, at 95 Irving, another Cambridge Historical

e. e. cummings

Commission plaque marks the house where **William James** (1842–1910), Henry's brother, lived between 1889 and 1910. Like Henry, the man heralded as the Father of Modern Psychology did not spend his early life in Cambridge. Born in New York City and raised in Europe and Newport, Rhode Island, William briefly pursued painting before entering Harvard Medical School and the world of science.

William James

In 1872, William James became a lecturer in physiology (1872–1873) and anatomy (1873–1876) at the medical school. While battling his own physical weakness and a nervous condition, James also battled the narrowness of Harvard's educational discipline, moving in and around the fields of medicine, physiology, philosophy, and psychology. In the lectures, articles, and books that he wrote over the next half century — such as *The Principles of Psychology* (1890), *Varieties of Religious Experience* (1902), *Pragmatism* (1907), and *A Pluralistic Universe* (1909) — James developed many of the concepts underlying modern psychology and philosophy, including pragmatism, radical empiricism, and stream of consciousness.

Continue on Irving Street to Kirkland, then turn right onto Kirkland and left onto Quincy. Passing Memorial Hall, continue on Quincy across Cambridge Street and Broadway. Take a right through the second gate into Harvard Yard, passing Emerson Hall on your left. This route was followed by Robert Lowell and commemorated in "T. S. Eliot" from "Writers" (*Notebook*, 1971):

Caught between two streams of traffic, in the gloom of Memorial Hall and Harvard's war-dead. . . . And he:

> The union of the mathematician with the poet, fervor with measure, passion with correctness, this surely is the ideal.
>
> — William James,
> *Collected Essays and Reviews* (1920)

*'Don't you loathe to be compared
with your relatives?
I do. I've just found two of mine
reviewed by Poe.
He wiped the floor with them . . .
and I was delighted.'*

Harvard Yard is impressive, both contemporary in its bustle and historic in its setting and structures. Equally impressive, however, is the number of graduates of international stature who have walked through here early in their educational journeys. The list of writers and thinkers who studied, taught, lectured, listened, argued, dropped out, or otherwise were affiliated with Harvard over the centuries is enough to fill several volumes.

Those graduates renowned for their writings would surely include Increase Mather (Class of 1656), Samuel Sewall (1671), Cotton Mather (1678), Thomas Prince (1707), Edward Everett

> Middlesex [County] is sacred territory, because it contains the city of Cambridge, home of Harvard, the center of the center and the hub of the hub.
>
> — Upton Sinclair, *Boston*

(1811), William Hickling Prescott (1814), George Bancroft (1817), Ralph Waldo Emerson (1821), Oliver Wendell Holmes (1829), John Lothrop Motley (1831), Theodore Parker (1836), Henry David Thoreau (1837), Richard Henry Dana, Jr. (1837), James Russell Lowell (1838), Francis Parkman (1844), Henry Adams (1858), William James (M.D., 1869), Owen Wister (1882), George Santayana (1886), Bernard Berenson (1887), W.E.B. Du Bois (1890), Van Wyck Brooks (1907), Samuel Eliot Morison (1908), T. S. Eliot (1909, A.M. 1911), Conrad Aiken (1912), Robert Benchley (1912), e. e. cummings (1915), J. P. Marquand (1915), John Dos Passos (1916), David McCord (1921), James Agee (1932), Daniel Boorstin (1934), Howard Nemerov (1941), Norman Mailer (1943),

Harvard Yard, 1871

Justin Kaplan (1945), Frank O'Hara (1950), Donald Hall (1951), Michael Halberstam (1953), John Updike (1954), Helen Vendler (Ph.D. 1960), and Michael Crichton (1964, M.D. 1969).

(Many women belong in this

AUTHOR / AUTHOR!

Julia Child on Irving Street and Fannie Farmer

I'm a Californian. In World War II, my husband, Paul, and I were in China, and Ceylon, and all kinds of places, and we decided rather than live in California, we would live in the Boston area where Paul grew up. I think that was 1956, and we bought the house on Irving Street for $35,000. It's the nicest neighborhood. It's easy to get to the Square. The house has a great big kitchen, and a great big room that Paul could use because he was a painter and woodcarver and photographer. Three of my TV series have been done in this kitchen.

It's an historic house that was built by Josiah Royce, a very famous philosopher in his time. Then e. e. cummings was across the street — Henry James lived two or three houses down — and, of course, we have the Schlesinger House up at the corner here. Around the corner is the famous John Kenneth Galbraith, on Francis Street. José Luis Sert, the architect, who was about five feet tall, lived about a block from the Galbraiths. One of the great neighborhood sights was seeing him and Galbraith — what is he, six-ten? — talking to each other.

This is a very free community and there are so many interesting people. In Concord we have the inspiration for the Culinary Historians of Boston, Barbara Wheaton. She's a marvelous person. Then you have that Schlesinger Library at Harvard, which has one of the best culinary collections in the country. The academics don't know much about the culinary arts or gastronomy, and you have to push them to show them this is a serious discipline.

Was I influenced by Fannie Farmer? I think she had an influence on everybody, because she was the first one who actually did measurements. I used her recipe for fudge when I was just a kiddie. Her *Boston Cooking-School Cook Book* was our cookbook, when I was way out in California! I visited her gravesite here at Mount Auburn. I still use her when I want to do real American cooking.

group. They appear later in the tour, when you visit Radcliffe College, the Schlesinger Archives, and the Bunting Fellowship.)

Meanwhile, talented writers in every discipline have also taught at Harvard. Among them are the ballad collector Francis James Child, the philosopher William James, the art historian Charles Eliot Norton, the poet and linguist Henry Wadsworth Longfellow, the scientist Louis Agassiz, the playwright George Pierce Baker, and the critic Helen Vendler. The screenwriter Spike Lee was a visiting lecturer, though only for a semester.

The Harry Elkins Widener Memorial Room, Widener Library

Pulitzer Prize–winning historians like Oscar Handlin, Samuel Eliot Morison, Bernard Bailyn, and Arthur M. Schlesinger, Jr., have taught at Harvard, as have Pulitzer Prize–winning poets like T. S. Eliot, Archibald MacLeish, Robert Lowell, Robert Frost, Elizabeth Bishop, and Seamus Heaney.

And the list goes on . . .

The most imposing structure in Harvard Yard is the **Harry Elkins Widener Memorial Library,** the largest academic library in the United States. Widener's gargantuan Corinthian columns and distinctive classical exterior were the choice of his mother, Eleanor Elkins Widener, who donated the library in memory of her son (Harvard class of 1907), who went down with the *Titanic* in 1912. Today, Widener holds some 50 miles of bookshelves and 3.5 million volumes.

Harvard's extensive library system — with Widener at its core — had humble beginnings. The original library was begun in 1638, when **John Harvard** (1607–1638) died, donating half his estate plus his personal collection of books — 329 titles in 400 volumes — to the two-year-old college. Over the next century, the library's holdings grew tenfold — then virtually disappeared overnight. In the Great Fire of January 24, 1764, most of the school's 5,000-volume library was lost. The happy exceptions were the 144 books checked out at the time, including only one from John Harvard's original library, *The Christian Warfare Against the Devil, World, and Flesh.*

Widener's immediate predecessor was Gore Hall (1841). A popular landmark perpetuated on the seal of the City of Cambridge, Gore Hall could barely keep up with the college's acquisitions. In 1877 an east wing was built, at a cost of $90,000, with six tiers of stacks that could hold 300,000 volumes. These were the first modern library stacks, where the bookshelves formed part of a metal framework resting directly on the building's foundation while supporting openwork floors and a roof.

Gore Hall was demolished in 1913 to make way for the vast Widener, which opened in 1915. Among its collections are a 1623 edition of Shakespeare's folios and a Gutenberg Bible.

Harvard College was responsible for producing the first version of the Bible ever printed in North America. In 1663, presses in Harvard's Indian College — a building on the Yard demolished in 1698 — created the 1,200-page Indian Bible, translated into the Algonquin dialect by "the

Apostle to the Indians" and Harvard graduate, the **Reverend John Eliot** (1604–1690).

According to Samuel Eliot Morison, the "Indian Bible" had trouble with words or concepts that had no Algonquin equivalent. The word for "virgin," for example, was either little used or little known. Hence, whenever it appeared in the text, Eliot replaced it with the closest word he could find, the Algonquin term for "a chaste young man."

Facing Widener, turn right and walk around to the front of University Hall.

Here is one of the Yard's most prized possessions: a bronze statue of the seated **John Harvard**, sculpted by Daniel Chester French in 1884. French is best

John Harvard, Harvard Yard

remembered for his *Minute Man* at the North Bridge in Concord, Massachusetts, his seated Lincoln, the centerpiece of the Lincoln Memorial in Washington, D.C., and *Death and the Sculptor,* at the entrance to Forest Hills Cemetery.

The popular John Harvard statue, inscribed "John Harvard, founder of Harvard College, 1638," has been dubbed "the Statue of Three Lies": (1) the image is not of Harvard, since no known rendering of him existed; French used Sherman Hoar of Concord, a student chosen at random, as a model; (2) Harvard College was founded in 1636, not 1638; and (3) John was not a founder of the college but its first benefactor, who, as noted before, donated his library and half of his estate to the school.

Directly across the way is **Massachusetts Hall**, where

> Strange interlude! Yes, our lives are merely strange dark interludes in the electrical display of God the Father.
>
> — Eugene O'Neill,
> *Strange Interlude*
> (1928)

George Pierce Baker taught his 47 Workshop in playwriting that was attended by nascent talents like Thomas Wolfe and Eugene O'Neill. Massachusetts Hall — which houses the university's president, provost, and vice-president — has not been used for classrooms since the turn of the last century.

Return to Harvard Square by taking any of the nearby paths through the brick gateways back to Mass. Ave.

Pick up the main route of the Literary Trail at the center of Harvard Square. Brattle Street begins across from the Out of Town newsstand, then takes an abrupt right in front of One Brattle Square. Just after the Brattle Theatre on the left is 42 Brattle, a yellow clapboard building that is now the Cambridge Center for Adult Education.

Blacksmith House, Cambridge Center for Adult Education

This is the **1727 Brattle House**, originally one of a series of Loyalist farms that stretched from here to Fresh Pond Parkway. The number of Loyalists who lived in spectacular Brattle Street homes during the revolutionary era gave Brattle the name of Tory Row. **Margaret Fuller**, a Cambridge native, feminist, transcendentalist, and editor of the *Dial*, lived here in 1832.

Ahead on the left and also part of the Cambridge Center for Adult Education, 54 Brattle Street was the home of Dexter Pratt, who was immortalized by his neighbor, the poet Henry Wadsworth Longfellow, in "The Village Blacksmith" (1839):

Under a spreading chestnut tree
The village smithy stands
The smith a mighty man he is
With large and sinewy hands,
And the muscles of his brawny arms
Are strong as iron bands.

Today, the **Blacksmith House** continues its literary connection as the home of the Blacksmith House Poetry Series. Founded in 1973 by Gail Mazur and sponsored by the Cambridge Center for Adult Education, this nationally known poetry series offers a variety of contemporary poetry and fiction programs. Readings by authors and poets, open to the public for a modest fee, are held on Monday evenings from October through May.

Farther down on the left is 60 Brattle Street, Harvard's **Loeb Drama Center** and the American Repertory Theater. Robert Brustein, its artistic director for many years, was elected to the American Academy of Arts and Sciences in 1999. An English professor at Harvard, he is also a drama critic for the *New Republic*, and the author of many books.

Continuing down Brattle Street, you will pass through part of the

Radcliffe Yard

Over the past century, countless writers have been affiliated with Radcliffe, including the inimitable Gertrude Stein (Class of 1898), the historical writer Barbara Tuchman (1933), the journalist and author Phyllis Schlafly (1945), the novelist Rona Jaffe (1951), the Canadian author Margaret Atwood (1962), the playwright Honor Moore (1967), and the feminist Susan Faludi (1981). Among Radcliffe's many poets are Maxine Kumin (1946, M.A., 1948), Adrienne Rich (1951), Phyllis Koestenbaum (1952), and Anne Sexton (Radcliffe Institute, 1961–1963).

Radcliffe College campus, now known as the Radcliffe Institute for Advanced Study, Harvard University. In 1879, Harvard's professors — who taught only men — were asked to make accommodations for instructing women as well. By 1894, the Society for the Collegiate Instruction for Women had been named Radcliffe College, after the donor of Harvard's first seventeenth-century endowment, Ann Radcliffe.

Among the significant buildings here are Agassiz House, named for **Elizabeth Cary Agassiz**, Radcliffe's first president, and Longfellow Hall, which honors **Alice Longfellow**. The eldest daughter of the poet, Alice was heavily involved in the development of education for women at Radcliffe.

On the corner of Brattle and James streets, behind the brick gate at 3 James, is the **Arthur and Elizabeth Schlesinger Library on the History of Women in America**, the home of the Radcliffe Archives. A variety of women scholars, writers, reformers, critics, and social activists have placed their papers here, including the classicist Edith Hamilton, the novelist of the Harlem Renaissance Dorothy West (*The Living Is Easy*), the playwright Eve Merriam, the feminists Charlotte Perkins Gilman (*The Yellow Wallpaper*), Betty Friedan, and Pauli Murray, the abolitionist Harriet Beecher Stowe, the novelist and social reformer Margaret Deland, and the poet and novelist Helen Hunt Jackson (*Mercy Philbrick's Choice*). The library also collects the papers of culinary artists, notably Julia Child, Irma Rombauer (*The Joy of Cooking*), and M.F.K. Fisher.

Directly across Brattle Street is the right-hand driveway of Greenleaf House, at 76 Brattle. Built in 1859 and once the home of Mary Longfellow and her husband, James Greenleaf, it became the official residence of Radcliffe presidents after 1913.

Follow the brick wall on the right down a small footpath to the rear to find a quiet treasure: a modest Roman fountain with a stream of water pouring from a lion's mouth into a tiled pool. On the ivy-covered wall behind is a pair of plaques — one in Braille, one in English — placed by **Helen Keller** (1880–1968), a Radcliffe alumna: *In memory of ANNE*

Helen Keller, Annie Sullivan, and Edward Everett Hale, 1903

SULLIVAN, teacher extraordinary — who, beginning with the word water, opened to the girl Helen Keller the world of sight and sound through touch. Beloved companion through Radcliffe College, 1900–1904.

Helen Keller was unable to see, hear, or speak since infancy. In *The Story of My Life* (1924), she explains how Sullivan taught her the word "water": *We walked down the path to the well-house, attracted by the fragrance of the honeysuckle with which it was covered. Some one was drawing water and my teacher placed my hand under the spout. As the cool stream gushed over one hand she spelled into the other the word water, first slowly, then rapidly. I stood still, my whole attention fixed upon the motions of her fingers. Suddenly I felt a misty consciousness as of something forgotten — a thrill of returning thought; and somehow the mystery of language was revealed to me. I knew then that "w-a-t-e-r" meant the wonderful cool something that was flowing over my hand. That living word awakened my soul, gave it light, hope, joy, set it free!*

At the intersection of Brattle and Mason, Ash Street veers off to the left. If you are on foot, walk down this shady and quietly elegant street, lined with sturdy white fences, old-growth arbors, brick sidewalks, and well-tended gardens. Just past Ash Street Place, on the left, a Cambridge Historical Commission plaque on 14 Ash notes that the poet **T. S. (Thomas Stearns) Eliot** (1888–1965), lived here in 1913 and 1914, while teaching philosophy at Harvard.

Eliot was already familiar with Harvard when he returned to lecture. A member of the Class of 1910, he graduated a year early, then went on to complete his master's degree by 1911. Though he could trace his ancestry back to colonial New England, Eliot was born to a poet and a businessman in St. Louis, Missouri. His poetic sensibility, however, required a different terrain than Cambridge had to offer, and he fled to England in 1914. There, Eliot found a bad marriage, Ezra Pound, a nervous breakdown, and the muses he had been seeking. Soon he wrote *Ezra Pound: His Metric and Poetry* (1917), *Prufrock and Other Observations* (1917), *Poems* (1920), *The Waste Land* (1922), and his first volume of criticism, *The Sacred Wood* (1920). When not writing reviews and poems — or finding fascination in the interplay of church and state — he periodically

> Poets in our civilization, as it exists at present, must be difficult. . . . The poet must become more and more comprehensive, more allusive, more indirect, in order to force, to dislocate if necessary, language into its meaning.
>
> — T. S. Eliot, *The Metaphysical Poets* (1921)

taught school, clerked in a bank, and edited literary journals. Though he became a British citizen, he returned to Harvard in 1932 — his first trip across the Atlantic since his departure. His lectures there became *The Use of Poetry and the Use of Criticism* (1933).

Eliot went on to become the twentieth century's most celebrated English-language poet and was awarded both the Nobel Prize for Literature and the British Order of Merit in 1948. Curiously, one of the poet's weakest works won him undying fame when, in 1981, the musical version of *Old Possum's Book of Practical Cats* (1939), opened on the London stage. The extravaganza called *Cats* has been a popular mainstay of American stages ever since.

> Immature poets imitate; mature poets steal.
>
> — T. S. Eliot, *Philip Massinger* (1920)

If the Old Corner Bookstore was *the* gathering place for mid-nineteenth-century writers in

Boston, the elegant home of **Henry Wadsworth Longfellow** (1807–1882) at 105 Brattle Street — today **Longfellow National Historic Site** — was an equally powerful magnet in Cambridge. Built in 1759 for the wealthy Tory John Vassall, Jr., this private house served as General Washington's headquarters for nine months in 1775 when he took charge of the Continental Army. In the 1830s, when the young Longfellow was hired to teach modern languages at Harvard, the house belonged to Elizabeth Craigie, the widow of Andrew Craigie. Longfellow first rented two rooms here in 1837. Six years later, Longfellow and his new wife, Fanny Appleton, were given the home as a wedding gift from Fanny's father.

One of the nineteenth century's most popular poets, scholars, and educators, Longfellow was a native of Portland, Maine. Two years after publishing his first poem, the fifteen-year-old joined Nathaniel Hawthorne's and Franklin Pierce's class at Bowdoin College, in Brunswick, Maine. His college work completed, Longfellow studied romance languages abroad, then returned to Bowdoin as its librarian and professor of modern languages before moving to Cambridge.

Once lodged in the Craigie mansion and at Harvard, Longfellow, along with his family and friends, proved integral to the development of American culture

Longfellow House with Henry Wadsworth Longfellow and his daughter Edith, circa 1870s

and traditions. The voluminous poetic works he completed during his forty-five years on Brattle Street include "The Courtship of Miles Standish," "The Village Blacksmith," "The Song of Hiawatha," "The Wreck of the Hesperus," and "Paul Revere's Ride."

The constant flow of Longfellow's international friends and guests included the finest thinkers and writers of his day — from his college classmate Nathaniel Hawthorne and the transcendentalist Ralph Waldo Emerson to the abolitionist Charles Sumner and many of Boston's most powerful citizens. Longfellow's wife, Fanny, was herself considered a noteworthy, though unpublished, art and literary critic.

To this assemblage Longfellow brought intellect, art, camaraderie, and joy. William Dean Howells, in *Literary Friends and Acquaintance* (1900), recalled his unique presence: *When he walked, he had kind of a spring in his gait, as if now and again a buoyant thought lifted him from the ground. It was fine to meet him coming down a Cambridge street; you felt that the encounter made you a part of literary history, and set you apart with him for the moment from the poor and mean.*

Longfellow's first wife, Mary Storer Potter, had a miscarriage and died after four years of marriage. Fanny Appleton died prematurely as well, from burns incurred in a tragic fire at their home. The familiar vision we have of Longfellow today — the gentle sage with the flowing white beard — was partly a result of that fire. Suffering burns on his face as he attempted to smother the flames on his beloved Fanny, he later hid his scars with facial hair.

Writing to Annie and James T. Fields in 1861, Hawthorne expressed his disbelief at the event: *How does Longfellow bear this terrible misfortune? How are his own injuries? . . . I cannot at all reconcile this calamity to my sense of fitness. One would think that there ought to have been no deep sorrow in a man like him; and now comes this blackest of shadows, which no sunshine hereafter can ever penetrate! I shall be afraid ever to meet him again; he cannot again be the man that I have known.*

The likable Longfellow was always careful to stand aside from the political storms of the era. He admired revolutionary heroes of the safe and distant past and deliberately chose to put his study in the bedroom once used by General George Washington. His close friendship with Charles Sumner, however, may have inspired him to write *Poems on Slavery* (1842). Few of his contemporaries criticized Longfellow or his work, save the enigmatic Edgar Allan Poe, who wrote off most Hub residents as provincial "Frogpondians."

Even though the interior of the Longfellow House is currently closed to visitors, the building is inspirational and the setting stunning: it provides grand views from Brattle Street and faces Longfellow Park, which slopes down to the

---

The atmosphere of the man [Longfellow] pervaded his surroundings and threw a glamour over everything. Even those who were most intimate at [his] house felt the indescribable influence of tenderness, sweetness, and calm which filled the place.

— Annie Adams Fields,
    Authors and Friends

river. When the house reopens, visitors can see its nineteenth-century furnishings, artwork, some ten thousand books, and the dining room table around which important literary figures once gathered. You can also imbibe the aura of a home linked to three centuries of history and a site that has inspired countless generations of writers.

In Longfellow's day, the park across the street offered him a clear view of the Charles. That view is long gone, alas, though the park is still a beautiful place to stroll and a favorite spot for picnickers and dog walkers. The long stretch of green off Brattle Street leads to a short staircase and a memorial below. There, a bust of Longfellow (1914) by Daniel Chester French is surrounded by a bas-relief by Henry Bacon that depicts six of Longfellow's heroes: Miles Standish, Sandalphon, the Village Blacksmith, the Spanish Student, Evangeline, and Hiawatha.

An excellent walking tour of literary Cambridge can be found in *Footprints on the Sands of Time: Longfellow's 19th Century Cambridge*. Published in 1996 by the Eastern National Park and Monument Association, it offers stellar insights, images, stories, and literary quotations from America's Golden Age of Literature.

Beyond the Longfellow House is 121 Brattle, the former home of **Joseph Worcester** (1784–1865).

Like Longfellow, Worcester was once a lodger at the widow Craigie's. He was the *other* dictionary-maker, renowned in the nineteenth century for his huge, unabridged *English Dictionary* (1843), which sought to standardize the English language and make it accessible to all. Today, Worcester's name is overshadowed by that of his contemporary Noah Webster, who developed *Webster's Dictionary*.

Continuing down Brattle Street, filled with majestic homes and grand yards, you will pass Sparks, Riedesel, and Appleton streets. Just past Appleton on the right, at 159 Brattle, is the **Hooper-Lee-Nichols House** (1680s; remodeled ca. 1760), the home of the Cambridge Historical Society. At 165 Brattle once lived the master of quotations, **John Bartlett** (1820–1905), when not at work in his University Book Store in Harvard Square.

Farther down Brattle Street, at 192, was the family home of **Josephine Preston Peabody** (1874–1922), and her husband, the Harvard professor Lionel Marks. Renowned as a poetic dramatist — whose plays included *Fortune and Men's Eyes* (1900), *Marlowe* (1901), *The Piper* (1909), and *Portrait of Mrs. W.* (1922) — Peabody saw her first poem printed in the *Atlantic* when she was nineteen. After attending Girls Latin School in Boston and Radcliffe College in

Cambridge, where she was a special student for two years, Peabody's first book, *Old Greek Folk Stories*, was published by Houghton Mifflin. From 1901 to 1903, she taught poetry and literature at Wellesley College. In her later years, Peabody was a crusader for liberal causes like women's suffrage, laborers' rights, pacifism, and relief for war refugees. She died at forty-eight, after a two-week coma brought on by hardening of the arteries to the brain.

Take a left off Brattle Street onto Elmwood and walk down to the large, elegant estate on the right, at 33 Elmwood. Now known as the **Oliver-Gerry-Lowell House**, this 1767 Tory mansion was once the home of Vice President Elbridge Gerry. Today it is the official residence of the president of Harvard.

Its most famous resident, however, was the poet, essayist, and diplomat **James Russell Lowell** (1819–1891), who spent his entire life at Elmwood. Lowell belonged to the New Eng-land Lowells, who, along with the Lawrences, ran much of

nineteenth-century New England. When not building textile mills or having towns northwest of Boston named in their honor, the Lowells produced their fair share of scholars, lawyers, clerics, and merchants.

James Russell Lowell had a number of careers open to him. After graduating from Harvard and choosing Maria White as his wife, he rejected medicine, the ministry, and the law to pursue literary and political writing, with an emphasis on poetry and abolitionism. Among his best works were four that were published in 1848: *Poems, The Vision of Sir Launfal, A Fable for Critics,* and *The Bigelow Papers*— the latter a witty satire on the wildly unpopular Mexican War. Lowell went on to influence and nurture other writers when he succeeded Longfellow as professor of Modern Languages at Harvard, became the first editor of the *Atlantic Monthly*, and an editor of the *North American Review*.

James Russell Lowell

Throughout his life, the distinctive house at 33 Elmwood, with its impressive double chimneys, was a gentle muse to Lowell:

My Elmwood chimneys seem croon-
ing to me,
As of old in their moody, minor key,
And out of the past the hoarse wind
blows.

Muses, of course, come and go. Like any other writer, Lowell endured large stretches of time when ideas rarely appeared, as noted in this letter, reprinted in *Memories of a Hostess* (1922): *From my study, this first day for three weeks without a drowsy pain in my knowledge box, I really feel a little lively, and wonder at myself. But*

don't be alarmed — it won't last,
any more than money does, or prin-
ciple in a politician, or hair, or pop-
ular favor — or paper.

Turn around and return to Brattle Street. To stay on the main route of the Literary Trail, bear right onto Brattle. To continue "Off the Beaten Path," take a left onto Brattle and follow it the few blocks to its end. Cross Mount Auburn Street to reach the neo-Egyptian entrance of Mount Auburn Cemetery.

Mount Auburn Cemetery

APPROXIMATE TIME: 1–3 HOURS

Cemeteries — like homes, bookshops, lecture halls, and hotels — were gathering places for the literary world of Boston. Certainly, friends came together at the funerals of beloved kith and kin. But they also often chose the same cemeteries, and sometimes the same sections of those cemeteries, for their eternal rest. As a result, there may be no larger gathering of late American literary figures than Mount Auburn Cemetery in Cambridge. Founded in 1831 as the first rural garden cemetery in America, Mount Auburn even had a literary beginning.

For many decades, the woods between the road to Watertown and the Charles River had been a popular site for Harvard students to wander and muse. Ralph Waldo Emerson and, years later, Robert Frost, walked here often, accompanied by a book or friend. Though properly known as Stone's Farm, the land was called "Sweet Auburn" by the students, after Oliver Goldsmith's poem "The Deserted Village" (1770):

*Sweet Auburn! loveliest village of
    the plain,
Where health and plenty cheer'd
    the labouring swain,
Where smiling spring its earliest
    visit paid,
And parting summer's lingering
    blooms delay'd:
Dear lovely bowers of innocence
    and ease,
Seats of my youth, when every
    sport could please,
How often have I loiter'd o'er thy
    green,
Where humble happiness endear'd
    each scene!*

When the land was purchased by a group of Bostonians and developed as a cemetery, the name Auburn remained. So too did the community's interest in wandering amid these wooded slopes while honoring their friends and heroes with tokens of remembrance.

From its earliest years, Mount Auburn Cemetery was the preferred resting place of hundreds of famous women and men. Maps of the cemetery, available for a nominal fee at the front gate and main office, note the location of many of these significant residents and their memorials. Audiotapes, both for driving and walking, can be rented or purchased at the front office as well.

Among the writers to be found here are many of the people we've met elsewhere on the Literary Trail, such as Henry Wadsworth Longfellow, Julia Ward Howe, James T. and Annie Fields, Fannie Farmer, Amy Lowell, James Russell Lowell, Francis Parkman, Oliver Wendell Holmes, John Bartlett, Hannah Adams, Josephine St. Pierre Ruffin, Isabella Stewart Gardner, and David McCord. Charles Little and James Brown are here too — the namesakes of Little, Brown publishers — with identical brownstone Gothic monuments on adjoining lots.

Most of these people lie below their finely sculpted monuments. Other markers, known as cenotaphs, are memorials to the dead that do not contain their earthly remains. Margaret Fuller (Ossoli), for example, was lost in a shipwreck with her husband and child. Though her baby was found and interred here, his parents' bodies were never recovered. The memorial to Robert Gould Shaw is a cenotaph as well, since his body remains in the mass grave at Fort Wagner, South Carolina, where he and his soldiers fell.

Other people of letters at Mount Auburn include Bernard Malamud (*Rembrandt's Hat*), R. Buckminster Fuller (*Synergetics*), Eleanor Hodgman Porter (*Pollyanna*), Thomas Bulfinch (*Bulfinch's Mythology*), and the founder of the Christian Science Church, Mary Baker Eddy, who wrote the essential book on spirituality and healing, *Science and Health with Key to the Scriptures* (1875).

Perhaps less familiar is Harriet Jacobs, whose autobiography, *Incidents in the Life of a Slave Girl: Written by Herself* (1861), was a groundbreaking

Cenotaph of Margaret Fuller, Mount Auburn Cemetery

and controversial work. Born into slavery in North Carolina, Jacobs escaped to the North and was hidden for years until her freedom was finally purchased in 1852.

Mount Auburn became such a prestigious address for its permanent residents that it was continually praised — and mocked — in both prose and poetry. Here, some long-forgotten bard muses about pompous landscapes in "A True Bostonian," a popular poem from the turn of the twentieth century:

A soul from Earth to Heaven went
To whom the Saint as he drew
*   near*
Said, "Sir, what claims do you
*   present,*
To us to be admitted here?"
"In Boston I was born and bred,
And in her schools was educated;
I afterwards at Harvard read,
And was with
*   honors grad-*
*   uated.*
In Trinity a pew
*   I owned*
Where Brooks is
*   held in such*
*   respect;*
And the society
*   is known*
To be the cream
*   of the select.*

In fair Nahant a charming spot,
I own a villa, lawn, arcades,
And last a handsome burial lot
In dead Mount Auburn's hallowed
*   shades."*
St. Peter mused, and shook his
*   head,*
Then as a gentle sigh he drew,
"Go back to Boston, friend," he
*   said,*
"Heaven isn't good enough for
*   you."*

It should be noted that degrees from Boston Latin and Harvard, a pew at Trinity Church, and a summer home at Nahant were not in the pedigree of most of Mount Auburn's occupants. Henry Wadsworth Longfellow is indeed buried here; so too is "The Village Blacksmith" about whom he wrote.

Mount Auburn Cemetery entrance

A brief foray into **Cambridge Cemetery**, next door, shows that not every literary Cantabrigian chose to spend the hereafter at Mount Auburn.

Leaving through the front gate of Mount Auburn, take a right onto Mount Auburn Street, then another right onto Coolidge Avenue. The main gate of Cambridge Cemetery is a half mile down the road on the left, marked by stone pillars. Maps of the cemetery are available at the office by the front gate, though they do not note specific graves.

Head up Summit Avenue and bear left onto the outer road of the cemetery, passing the playing fields of Shady Hill and the Buckingham, Browne & Nichols schools. Curve back onto Prospect Avenue to find two similar lots, both backed by low red brick walls. One marks William Dean Howells and his family, the other the Jameses, including William, Henry, and Alice.

Thomas Wentworth Higginson, the correspondent of Emily Dickinson, is buried at the junction of Riverview, Lawn, and Prospect. Sadly, the site seems forgotten, for it is crowded by such useful items as a faucet and trash can.

Sic transit gloria mundi . . .

If you have traveled as far as Mount Auburn and Cambridge cemeteries, return to Brattle Street and walk back toward Harvard Square. Take a left at Appleton Street, then a right onto Brewster. A Cambridge Historical Commission plaque notes that 35 Brewster, a wide double house, was the home of **Robert Frost** (1874–1963) for the last two decades of his life.

Though born in San Francisco, Robert Frost became known as the quintessential New England poet. After years of different activities — from bobbin- and shoe-making to teaching and farming — Frost moved to England and published his first book of poems, *A Boy's Will* (1913). After his successful publication of *North of Boston* in 1914, Frost was on his way back to America — and on his way to being recognized as a significant American poet.

In his writing, Frost was not particularly innovative. When asked what he thought of free verse in an interview with *Newsweek* in 1957, he replied, "I'd just as soon play tennis with the net down." Still, Frost broke through the transcendentalist and Victorian values of the nineteenth century to write with a modern sensibility in plain, readable rhyme. His best lines were

Robert Frost

multilayered, deeply American, and emotionally restrained. They touched the hearts and minds of generations of Americans — and made Frost the logical choice to speak at John F. Kennedy's inauguration in 1961.

Like Longfellow a century before him, Frost became the nation's most recognized and honored man of poetry. He was awarded countless prizes, including Pulitzers for *New Hampshire* (1924), *Collected Poems* (1931), *A Further Range* (1937), and *A Witness Tree* (1943). Only his circle of friends knew of his fierce competitiveness and — in his later years — eccentric irritability. One night in 1938, for example, Frost set fire to a stack of papers to disrupt a poetry reading by Archibald MacLeish.

Frost taught at Amherst College between 1916 and 1938. After the death of his wife, he moved to 88 Mount Vernon Street, overlooking Louisburg Square. Then, after his son's suicide, Frost's friends and fans formed the Ralph Waldo Emerson poetry fellowship at Harvard and enticed the poet to lecture in Harvard's English Department. Frost bought the left half of this house on Brewster Street in 1941 and lived here when not staying in Vermont or Florida.

Walk to the end of Brewster and take a right onto Sparks Street, then a hard left onto Craigie at the large intersection. Take a quick left down Buckingham Street, past the elementary school campus of the private Buckingham, Browne & Nichols School.

Perched on a hill on the left, 29 Buckingham was the home of **Thomas Wentworth Higginson** (1823–1911), whose many roles included author, essayist, aboli-

I shall be telling this with a sigh
Somewhere ages and ages
    hence:
Two roads diverged in a wood,
    and I —
I took the one less traveled by,
And that has made all the
    difference.

— Robert Frost, *The Road
    Not Taken* (1916)

Thomas Wentworth Higginson, 1903

tionist, minister, Civil War officer, and correspondent of Emily Dickinson. Born in Cambridge, the precocious, happy, and well-read Higginson entered Harvard at thirteen, was elected to Phi Beta Kappa at sixteen, graduated at seventeen, then went on to Harvard Divinity School. Though he entered the ministry — tending flocks in Newburyport and, later, Worcester, Massachusetts — he proved a radical nonconformist and inveterate man of action.

While many of his literary peers of the 1850s opposed slavery, most were content to document their concerns in books, journals, lectures, and petitions. Hence, in 1854, when an escaped slave named Anthony Burns was arrested in

Boston — and threatened with extradition to his southern master under the Fugitive Slave Law — Richard Henry Dana offered to defend Burns in court, while the pacifist poet John Greenleaf Whittier called for nonviolent resistance.

Higginson's response was singular. Not satisfied with the slow course of justice, he led a small group of radicals and stormed the U.S. Courthouse in Boston armed with a huge battering ram, axes, revolvers, and butcher's cleavers. Though their mission failed — and Burns was returned to slavery, at least for a time — Higginson received a saber slash on his chin that he displayed proudly for the rest of his life.

Higginson continued his life of left-wing politics and adamant action by backing the efforts of John Brown and leading a regiment of black soldiers in the Civil War. Returning home, he filled his days with writing, teaching, and a perennial commitment to social reform — especially equal rights for blacks and women. Among his works are *Army Life in a Black Regiment* (1870), biographies of Margaret Fuller (1884), Whittier (1902), and Longfellow (1902), and a fascinating autobiography, *Cheerful Yesterdays* (1898).

Higginson is best known, however, for his literary relationship with **Emily Dickinson** (1830–

> If I feel physically as if the top of my head were taken off, I know that is poetry.
>
> — Emily Dickinson, cited in Thomas Wentworth Higginson, "Emily Dickinson's Letters," *Atlantic Monthly*, October 1891

1886). In 1862, the self-proclaimed Belle of Amherst wrote to Higginson after reading one of his articles in the *Atlantic*. She began her letter, "Mr. Higginson — are you too deeply occupied to say if my verse is alive?" Higginson puzzled over her "remarkable, though odd" form and content, then advised the young poet not to publish. Their correspondence continued over the next two decades, filled with encouragement and fondness. The reclusive, brilliant Dickinson sent Higginson a poem with every letter. It was not until after her death that her sister Lavinia and Mabel Loomis Todd, the wife of an Amherst professor, contacted Higginson anew and convinced him to help them publish the poems. Even then, Higginson felt compelled to alter some of the poet's rhyme, rhythm, lines, language, and punctuation — an error not corrected for many decades.

Though Dickinson is not usually associated with Boston or Cambridge, she did travel here twice during the Civil War era. In 1864 she stayed in Cambridgeport while seeing an eye specialist, Dr. Henry Williams, and in 1865 she returned for six months of treatments. Once home, however, she never left Amherst again.

Take Healy Street, on the right near Higginson's old home, to Parker, then turn right toward Buckingham in order to return to Craigie Street. As you drive along Craigie, you'll pass the private Craigie Circle on your left.

Vladimir Nabokov (1899–1977) lived at 8 Craigie Circle between 1942 and 1948. Nabokov came from a wealthy Russian family, which fled from their homeland toward the end of the Russian Revolution. Educated at Trinity College in Cambridge, England, Nabokov moved to America in 1940, became a U.S. citizen in 1945, and taught at Wellesley, then Cornell. His extraordinary lectures on Russian and European literature only ended when his success at

> For me a work of fiction exists only insofar as it affords me what I shall bluntly call aesthetic bliss.
>
> — Vladimir Nabokov, *On a Book Entitled Lolita* (1956)

writing allowed him to retire from the lectern.

Among Nabokov's many stylized and witty novels are *Laughter in the Dark* (1938), *The Real Life of Sebastian Knight* (1941), and *Lolita* (1958). His stories, poems, and lectures have also appeared in collected form. While living in Cambridge in the 1940s, Nabokov worked part-time at Harvard's Museum of Comparative Zoology. Since then, critics have dissected his works, seeking and analyzing his references to butterflies.

Continue along Craigie Street and take a left onto Concord Avenue at the intersection. Just ahead on the left is 34 Concord, the **Mary Ingraham Bunting Fellowship Program of the Radcliffe Institute for Advanced Study**, an international multidisciplinary center. Each year some forty fellows, working in a community setting, pursue projects that make significant contributions in their fields. Among the twelve hundred Bunting alumnae are the playwright Paula Vogel, the journalist

---

AUTHOR / AUTHOR!

Anne Bernays on Literary Mist in Cambridge

It's difficult to live in Cambridge without acknowledging writers long gone whose essence adheres like the perfume they used to spray at you in expensive department stores.

Whether or not your own prose is anything like theirs, you feel an obligation to succeed at some level for their sake. Around the corner from where I live is the house of e. e. cummings, whose poetry, when I read it first in college, struck me as astonishing with its cubist syntax and deliberately skewed vision. It still seems fresh and minty.

Henry James, by any standard a towering figure for novelists, lived in Cambridge as a young man. Although he left thereafter, you can feel New England in his bones, even when he's writing about New Yorkers or Europeans. James burrowed into nuances of human temperament and reaction in a way you can only envy and try, palely, to emulate.

It's nice to think of Vladimir Nabokov sitting in a musty room at Harvard's Peabody Museum down the street, cataloguing his beloved butterflies. For me, Nabokov is the supreme prose artist of the twentieth century. To read one page of, say, *Speak, Memory,* is to be fueled for a week. *Lolita,* satire and love story, is matchless; *Pnin* a model of sweet humor.

Christina Robb, the historian Nell Painter, and the writers Alice Walker, Jayne Anne Phillips, Gish Jen, Sue Miller, Tillie Olsen, and Fae Myenne Ng. The poets Maxine Kumin, Patricia Cleary Miller, Jorie Graham, and Anne Sexton were also once Bunting fellows.

Across the street, at 37 Concord Avenue, is the home of **William Dean Howells** (1837–1920), America's preeminent man of letters at the turn of the last century. Well known as the gentleman who replaced James T. Fields as editor of the *Atlantic Monthly*, Howells was also a novelist, poet, essayist, short story writer, and critic of considerable talent. His finest novel, *The Rise of Silas Lapham* (1885), is the classic account of the nouveau riche post–Civil War industrialist who couldn't buy his way into the culture of Boston Brahmins. *Silas Lapham*, as it turns out, portrayed a microcosm of Howell's ambivalent feelings about Boston and Bostonians.

Born in Ohio, Howells came to Boston in search of a literary mecca. In 1860, the twenty-three-year-old writer took a stagecoach to Concord, Massachusetts, and proceeded to introduce himself to Hawthorne, Thoreau, and Emerson. As fate would have it, the man who first sought literary culture in Boston eventually helped mold it. By 1866 he was an assistant editor

at the *Atlantic* and by 1871, chief editor.

Howells became a magnet for other writers, both local and national. He befriended the James family as well as Oliver Wendell Holmes, James Russell Lowell, Charles Eliot Norton, and Longfellow. He introduced the western writers Mark Twain and Bret Harte to the Saturday Club and came to live in all the right places — including Beacon Street and Louisburg Square in Boston, and Sacramento Street and Concord Avenue in Cambridge.

Howells was such an important literary figure in Boston that many historians equate his departure for New York in 1881 with the end of Boston as the literary hub of America. Surely Howells sensed that the center for books, magazines, and literature was starting to shift to Manhattan. Moreover, the intellectual institutions that drew him here in the first place — Harvard College, the Boston Athenaeum, and the *Atlantic Monthly* — could not offset his concerns about the new people he saw coming to Boston and Cambridge.

"All Ireland seems to be poured upon [us]," Howells wrote to Henry James in 1869, "and there is such a clamor of Irish children about us all day, that I suspect my 'exquisite English,' as I've seen it called in the papers, will yet be written with a brogue." This xenophobia and condescension that Howells and James shared toward Boston's new immigrant populations was, sadly, not unique among their peers.

The Literary Trail now moves from Cambridge to Concord.

To get to the town of Concord, follow Concord Avenue to Route 2, past Fresh Pond. The paths and areas around the pond here are a favorite spot for joggers, walkers (with and without dogs), and bicyclists today. Almost a century ago, William Dean Howells and Henry James used to walk together here as well, discussing their work while watching the skaters — or boaters — on the pond, depending on the season.

Pass the Alewife "T" station, then bear left and continue on Route 2, now a highway. At the second set of lights after crossing I-95/128, where Route 2 takes a sharp left, continue straight ahead toward the center of Concord on the Cambridge Turnpike.

As you travel down this old Cambridge Turnpike, you are taking the route that Ralph Waldo Emerson and his friends rode — by carriage or stagecoach — on their regular outings to Lexington, Cambridge, and Boston. In the first decades of the nineteenth century, the stage from Concord to Boston took three hours in good weather, up to five hours in bad. When the railroad was built in 1844, it shortened the trip to an hour and became the writers' preferred mode of transportation.

Crossing the Mill Brook, you will see the Concord Museum on the right. Stop near the gazebo outside the museum, just before the intersection with Lexington Road. Directly across the street is the house where Emerson lived from 1835 until his death in 1882.

I walk along the Mill Brook below Emerson's, looking into it for some life. . . . Perhaps what most moves us in winter is some reminiscence of far-off summer. How we leap by the side of the open brooks! What beauty in the running brooks! What life! What society! The cold is merely superficial; it is the summer still at the core, far, far within.

— Henry David Thoreau, *Journal*

Concord

HOUGH SETTLED IN 1635 as the first inland town in Massachusetts, charming Concord, sixteen miles northwest of Boston, first gained international repute in 1775. On the morning of April 19, patriot minute men fought off the British regulars on Concord's North Bridge — "the shot heard round the world" that marked the start of the American Revolution. By the middle of the nineteenth century, however, the grandchildren and great-grandchildren of those early patriots were ready to play a central role in another revolution, albeit a quieter and gentler one. This rebellion involved the worlds of literature and ideas, and spawned two generations of intellectuals committed to social reform, spiritual uplift, and literary innovation.

> [Concord?] I think wise men and excellent women have no right to live elsewhere . . .
>
> — Bronson Alcott, *Journal*

Today, you can still visit the beautifully maintained homes, studies, woods, and ponds — and bask in the warmth of the historic village — that once attracted some of the nineteenth century's greatest writers and thinkers.

The role of **Ralph Waldo Emerson** (1803–1882) in particular cannot be overemphasized when discussing literary Concord. The man known as "Concord's First Citizen" and "the Sage of Concord" was actually born and raised in Boston. Still, Concord was clearly Emerson's ancestral — not to mention his spiritual — home. Peter Bulkeley, Emerson's grandfather seven generations back, arrived in 1635 to help found Concord and become its first minister. Grandfather William Emerson was another family minister, who reportedly observed and wrote about the revolutionary activities on the North Bridge in April 1775. The Reverend Emerson's vantage point was The Old Manse, which he had built five years earlier.

Young Waldo — as Ralph Waldo Emerson was called by his friends

Concord Tour

1 Concord Museum
2 Ralph Waldo Emerson house
3 The Wayside
4 Orchard House
5 Concord Town Center
  Monument Square
  Civil War Memorial
  Concord Town House
6 Sleepy Hollow Cemetery

7 Monument Street
  The Old Manse
  North Bridge
8 Concord Town Center
  Colonial Inn
  Masonic Lodge Building
  Site of the old Concord Jail
9 Concord Free Public Library
10 Thoreau-Alcott house
11 Concord Depot
12 Walden Pond State Reservation

— followed his family's traditional pattern of education. He attended Boston Latin School, Harvard College, and Harvard Divinity School, and was ordained as the minister of Boston's Second Church (Unitarian) in 1829. That church was descended from the First Church of Boston, where Increase and Cotton Mather held forth during colonial times and Grandfather William more recently.

By 1832, however, Emerson's life was in turmoil. His young wife, Ellen Louisa Tucker, had died after only seventeen months of marriage. At the same time, his emerging personal philosophy about God was already in conflict with the Unitarian position, leading him to resign from the Second Church and ultimately from the ministry altogether. In December of that year, he sailed off to Europe, where he met with eminent British men of letters such as Thomas Carlyle, William Wordsworth, and Samuel Taylor Coleridge.

Back in Boston, Emerson em- barked on a new life of lecturing, writing, and embracing dissident New Englanders like himself. He also began replacing traditional Christian doctrines with a new philosophy called transcendental- ism. The old concept of God was replaced by the "Over-Soul," and each person was encouraged to lis- ten to his or her own inner voice while seeking the balance and unity within Nature.

By 1834, Emerson had moved to Concord, staying first at his fami- ly's home (later called The Old Manse by Hawthorne), then, by the following year, in a house he pur- chased on the Cambridge Turn- pike. **Emerson's house**, now a museum owned by his descendants, still stands at the intersection of the old turnpike and Lexington Road today. Why did Emerson choose to make his home in Concord? In part, it was his ancestral home. Another part, however, was surely the beautiful and tranquil natural landscape, still apparent today. As he noted in a *Journal* entry of 1846:

I think we escape something by living in the villages. In Concord here there is some milk of life, we are not so raving dis- tracted with wind and dyspepsia. The mania takes a milder form. People go a- fishing, and know the

Nineteenth-century view of Concord by J. W. Barber

What Was Transcendentalism?

Transcendentalism combined religion, philosophy, mysticism, and ethics. Transcendentalists believed that:

- All living things were bound together;
- Humans were essentially good;
- Insight was more powerful than experience as a source of knowledge.

The birth of American transcendentalism dates from 1836, when a group of people — many of them Unitarian ministers — met in the Boston home of George Ripley to discuss German philosophy and social issues of the day. The Transcendental Club, as it was called, met periodically, with a fluid roster of members.

These men and women lived all over New England. They conversed by mail, as well as in meetings and private visits — most frequently in Boston and Concord.

— *courtesy the Concord Museum*

taste of their meat. They cut their own whippletree in the woodlot, they know something practically of the sun and the east wind, of the underpinning and the roofing of the house, of the pan and the mixture of the soils.

In the course of his life here, Emerson's person, intellect, and home became beacons for a wealth of creative talent and literary genius from both near and far. Like Longfellow's home and Harvard College in Cambridge, or the Old Corner Bookstore and the Elizabeth Peabody Book Shop in Boston, the Emerson homestead served as a vital gathering place for the most fertile minds of mid-nineteenth-century America.

Emerson's friend and neighbor Louisa May Alcott, in an article for *The Youth's Companion*, described the aura and appeal of Emerson's home: *The marble walk that leads up to [Emerson's] door has been trodden by the feet of many pilgrims from all parts of the world, drawn thither by their love and reverence for him. In that famous study, his townspeople have had the privilege of seeing many of the great and good men and women of our time, and learning of their gracious host the finest lessons of true courtesy. I have often seen him turn from distinguished guests, to say a wise or kindly word to some humble worshipper sitting modestly in a corner, content merely to look and listen, and who went away to cherish that memorable moment long and gratefully.*

Despite his love for Concord and the crowds that gathered around him there, Emerson was well known for hopping into horse-drawn coaches or onto cars of the Fitchburg Railroad (which still makes regular trips from the Concord Depot into Boston). He was also a popular lecturer and traveled widely to deliver his wisdom, interwoven by what Annie Fields called a "furtive humor." In his lifetime, Emerson gave close to fifteen hundred lectures, some nine hundred in Massachusetts alone.

The **Concord Museum**, at the intersection of Lexington Road and the Cambridge Turnpike, is the logical first stop on a visit to Concord. Founded in 1886 and based on a well-documented collection of Americana begun by

Ralph Waldo Emerson's study

Cummings Davis in the 1850s, it offers a visual encyclopedia of Concord history.

A nationally significant collection of historical and literary artifacts, seventeenth- through nineteenth-century decorative arts galleries, and finely furnished period rooms featuring Concord clocks, furniture, and silver are only part of the museum's broad appeal. A new film called *Exploring Concord* and engaging galleries that answer the frequent question *Why Concord?* help to explain how the events in this small Massachusetts town had such a large impact on the world.

In the self-guided *Why Concord?* exhibition, town history is introduced with the Algonkian natives and the English settlers who lived with them in peace and "concord." The *Defending Concord* gallery focuses on the events that led to the start of the American Revolution in Lexington and Concord, including one of the original lanterns hung at

> Make much of your own place. The stars & celestial awning that overhang our simple Concord walks and discourses are as brave as those that were visible to Coleridge as he talked or to Dryden or Ben Jonson & Shakespeare or Chaucer & Petrarch & Boccaccio when they met.
>
> — Ralph Waldo Emerson, *Journal,* 1835

> I like to be in your library when you are out of it. It seems a sacred place. I came here to find a book, that I might feel more life and be worthy to sleep, but there is so much soul here I do not need a book . . .
>
> — Margaret Fuller, letter to Ralph Waldo Emerson, 1842

the Old North Church the night of Paul Revere's "midnight ride."

Of course, the great nineteenth-century writers who brought together Boston, Cambridge, and Concord are given appropriate play. Two of Concord's leading figures — Ralph Waldo Emerson and Henry David Thoreau — enjoy prominent places at the museum.

Though best known for his sojourn at Walden Pond and the book that followed, Thoreau was also a naturalist, inventor, civil engineer, social critic, and philosopher. Among the many personal possessions in the Thoreau gallery are the desk Thoreau used when writing *Civil Disobedience* and *Walden*, the walking stick that he used on his excursions, a manuscript from his lyceum lecture notes (published as the essay *Walking*), the bedstead from the cabin on Walden Pond, and pencils he

improved at his family's pencil factory.

The entire study of transcendentalist philosopher, essayist, Unitarian minister, and popular lecturer Emerson is here as well. Arguably the most influential thinker of his time, this proponent of individualism and self-reliance greeted a constant stream of visitors in his study while assembling such works as his *Essays* and *Poems*. The furnishings here were moved from the Emerson House, diagonally across the street, when the museum was built on part of the Emerson apple orchard in 1930.

At the corner, bear right off the Cambridge Turnpike onto Lexington Road. This is part of the Battle Road of American Revolutionary fame. Running parallel to it for almost a mile, stretching behind

The Wayside

some beautiful old homes, is the heavily wooded **Revolutionary Ridge**.

It's interesting to note that the writers in Concord who were part of America's nineteenth-century literary revolution were also attuned to the political revolution of the previous century. Many of them wrote stories or poems based on America's War for Independence, such as Hawthorne's *Septimius Felton*, Louisa May Alcott's *Tabby's Tablecloth*, and Emerson's "Concord Hymn." Meanwhile, the Revolution provided literary fodder for their friends in Boston and Cambridge as well, most notably "Paul Revere's Ride" (1863) by Longfellow:

Listen, my children, and you shall hear,
Of the midnight ride of Paul Revere,
On the eighteenth of April, in Seventy-five;
Hardly a man is now alive
Who remembers that famous day and year.

Farther down the street, at 455 Lexington Road, is **The Wayside**.

Nathaniel Hawthorne, 1846 crayon and chalk drawing by Eastman Johnson

(A parking lot across the way allows visits to both The Wayside and Orchard House.) The quaint Wayside is known as the only National Historic Landmark to have been the home of three writers — Nathaniel Hawthorne, Louisa May Alcott, and Harriett Lothrop. Well over three hundred years old, it was also the first literary site to become part of the National Park Service.

Nathaniel Hawthorne (1804–1864) was descended from one of New England's oldest families. The Hathornes — as the name was originally spelled — were legislators, magistrates, soldiers, and sailors long associated with the town of Salem, northeast of Boston. One particular ancestor, Judge John Hathorne, participated in the Salem witch trials of 1692 — a source of guilt that affected the young writer and surely influenced his works, including *The House of Seven Gables* and *The Scarlet Letter*.

It was perhaps a telling sign that Hawthorne was born on July 4 on the twenty-eighth anniversary of America's independence. In his

UTOPIAN COMMUNITIES

During the nineteenth century, idealized agrarian communes were created as experimental sites for cooperative living. Their goals included developing socially progressive thought — like socialism and transcendentalism — and implementing their principles in everyday life. In the Greater Boston area, the best-known communities were George Ripley's **Brook Farm** in West Roxbury, and Bronson Alcott's New Eden at **Fruitlands**, in the town of Harvard.

Like founder George Ripley, a large number of the participants in Brook Farm Institute of Agriculture and Education (1841–1847) were past or present members of the Unitarian Church who had come to espouse transcendentalist philosophies. Many of the area's most fertile minds — from Nathaniel Hawthorne, John Sullivan Dwight, and Charles Dana to Ralph Waldo Emerson, Margaret Fuller, and Horace Greeley — were either members or visitors to George and Josephine Ripley's renowned community. Though the intellectual life there was vibrant and the school excellent, economics played a major part in Brook Farm's demise: these thinkers were not skilled farmers, and the soil inadequate for good crop growth.

Far shorter-lived than Brook Farm was the New Eden at Fruitlands, founded by Bronson Alcott and Charles Lane in 1843, and ended later that winter. Known and loved as a brilliant, impractical transcendentalist, Alcott moved his wife and daughters to Fruitlands to share in farming the land, communing with nature, and engaging in intellectual exchanges. As it turned out, Bronson's wife, Abigail May, was left with the impossible task of holding the physical ship together as Bronson and his handful of fellow thinkers — including, at times, Thoreau and Emerson — spent more hours sailing on philosophical waters.

Though its site is listed on the National Register of Historic Places, no park or museum commemorates Brook Farm, located at 670 Baker Street, West Roxbury. Nathaniel Hawthorne used Brook Farm as the setting for his novel, *The Blithedale Romance* (1852).

Fruitlands, at 102 Prospect Hill Road in Harvard, is still a delightful place to visit. Purchased and saved by author and preservationist **Clara Endicott Sears** (1863–1960), the scenic, rolling hillsides here were opened to the public in 1914, and evolved into what is now known as the Fruitlands Museums. In addition to Bronson Alcott's old Farmhouse — which contains some interesting transcendentalist memorabilia — guests can enjoy a Shaker Museum, an Indian Museum, a Picture Gallery featuring landscapes from the Hudson River School and early folk art portraits, as well as a tea room, picnic space, and nature trails.

teen years, he declared his own independence from his family's past by deciding to become a writer. His seafaring father had died when the boy was just four, giving him a tendency toward solitude, somberness, and shy reserve that stayed with him throughout his life. An impressionable year of quiet near a favorite Maine lake was followed by his years at Bowdoin College, where he was a classmate of Longfellow and Franklin Pierce, the future U.S. president, who was a lifelong friend.

In the dozen years before publishing *The Scarlet Letter* (1850), Hawthorne spent several months in the experimental commune at Brook Farm in West Roxbury, married Sophia Peabody of Salem, worked at the custom house in both Salem and Boston, and lived in The Old Manse in Concord, collecting the stories that became *Mosses from an Old Manse* (1846). The success of *The Scarlet Letter* allowed Nathaniel and Sophia to spend 1850–1852 in Lenox, tucked into the beautiful Berkshires of western Massachusetts. It was an especially prolific period for him; he produced *The House of the Seven Gables* (1851), *The Snow Image and Other Twice-Told Tales* (1851), and *The Blithedale Romance* (1852), and began an intense friendship with Herman Melville (*Moby-Dick*), who adored Hawthorne and dedicated

his masterpiece to him.

In 1852, the family returned to Concord and settled into **The Wayside**, the only home that Hawthorne ever owned. Before he called it "Wayside," the Alcotts had named it "Hillside" when they owned it from 1845 to 1852. Many of the childhood events Louisa described in *Little Women*, including her amateur plays, occurred at Hillside. As it happened, The Wayside was saved by a later owner, **Harriett Mulford Stone Lothrop** (1844–1924), who made her own literary reputation as Margaret Sidney, creator of the *Five Little Peppers* children's books.

The main structure of The Wayside is a colonial farmhouse, although each family made its own distinctive additions. The east chamber, for example, is colonial, but Bronson Alcott added wings and porches, among other changes. The unique three-story tower was added by Hawthorne; his study on its top floor still holds his writing desk, murals painted in tribute to him, and his bookcases. Hawthorne's shaving stand is one of the original artifacts on display. Other interesting exhibits are shown in the adjacent barn.

James T. Fields, in *Yesterdays With Authors* (1871), mused on Hawthorne's life at The Wayside: *I saw him frequently at the Wayside, in Concord. He now seemed happily in the dwelling he had put in order for the calm and comfort of his middle and later life. He had added a tower to his house, in which he could be safe from intrusion, and where he could muse and write. Never was a poet or romancer more fitly shrined ... Shut up in his tower, he could escape from the tumult of life, and be alone with only the birds and the bees in concert outside his casement.*

Hawthorne himself was a little more dubious about the dwelling he had "put in order," as amusingly recalled in his *Letters: I have been equally unsuccessful in my architectural projects; and have transformed a simple and small old farm-house into the absurdest anomaly you ever saw; but I really was not so much to blame here as the village-carpenter,* *who took matters into his own hands, and produced an unimaginable sort of thing instead of what I asked for. ... I was given over to Satan, surely, when I first had to do with carpenters and painters.*

The house most closely associated with *Little Women* is **Orchard House**, at 399 Lexington Road, a short walk from The Wayside. In 1857 it was purchased by **Amos Bronson Alcott** (1799–1888), one of the most brilliant and unworldly of all the Concord transcendentalists. A great philosopher and teacher, sincere utopian, and decidedly impractical visionary, Alcott was considered a singularly excellent man. "It is impossible to quarrel with [Bronson Alcott]," observed Hawthorne, "for he would take all your harsh words like a saint."

The self-taught son of a Connecticut farmer, Alcott moved to Boston with his young wife in 1828. Blending romantic ideas about the goodness of mankind with idiosyncratic educational thought, he set up a series of progressive schools in Connecticut, Pennsylvania, and Massachusetts. Among his well-respected experiments was the Temple School in Boston, the communal experiment at Fruitlands, in Harvard, Massachusetts, and the Concord School of Philosophy — the last, a pioneering summer school for adult education. Though Alcott was con-

Bronson Alcott

INDEPENDENCE DAY

The Fourth of July seems to have taken on a special significance in the literary and sociopolitical history of Greater Boston. Nathaniel Hawthorne, for example, was born on Independence Day in 1804. July 4, 1829, was the day William Lloyd Garrison made his first antislavery speech at the Park Street Church in Boston; two years later, at the same spot, the song "America" made its debut. It was on Independence Day, 1837, that Ralph Waldo Emerson's "Concord Hymn" was first sung at the completion of the Battle Monument next to the North Bridge, and on Independence Day in 1845 that Henry David Thoreau moved into his cabin on Emerson's land by Walden Pond.

In September 1837, Emerson delivered an address at Harvard College that came to be called America's "*intellectual* Declaration of Independence." In this "American Scholar" speech, he noted: "*The scholar is the delegated intellect. In the right state he is* Man Thinking. . . . *Meek young men grow up in libraries, believing it their duty to accept the views which Cicero, which Locke, which Bacon have given, forgetful that Cicero, Locke and Bacon were only young men in libraries when they wrote these books.*"

In 1975, the Pulitzer Prize–winning poet Archibald MacLeish published *The Great American Fourth of July Parade*, which imagined Presidents John Adams and Thomas Jefferson commenting on the State of the Union in the 1970s. Adams — who, with his wife, Abigail, lived in Boston as well as Quincy — corresponded with Jefferson for many years and was a close friend. In 1813 Adams wrote: "You and I ought not to die, before we have explained ourselves to each other." Thirteen years later — on July 4, 1826, the fiftieth anniversary of the Declaration of Independence they had created together — Jefferson and Adams both died, each unaware of the other's demise.

stantly short of cash, he was able to buy Orchard House for his wife, Abigail May, and their daughters Anna, Louisa, Elizabeth, and May, with a little help from some devoted friends. From 1880 to shortly before his death, he ran his Concord School of Philosophy from the Hillside Chapel behind the house.

The main house was created from one eighteenth- and one seventeenth-century structure, which Alcott joined, improved, and vigorously landscaped. The writer Lydia Maria Child, after first visiting Orchard House, was impressed with its architectural integrity and decided quirks. In a letter to Mrs. S. B. Shaw in 1876, Child wrote: *The house of the Alcotts took my fancy greatly. . . . Mr. Alcott has an architectural taste more intelligible than his Orphic sayings. He let every old rafter and beam stay in its place, changed old ovens and ash-holes into Saxon-arched alcoves, and added a wash-woman's old shanty to the rear. The result is a house full of queer nooks and corners, and all manner of juttings in and out. It seems as if the spirit of some old architect had brought it from the Middle Ages and dropped it down in Concord.*

Louisa May Alcott, circa 1858

Still, it was not Bronson but his daughter **Louisa May Alcott** (1832–1888) who brought everlasting fame to Orchard House. Born in Germantown, Pennsylvania, Louisa was an independent spirit. Though she held a variety of jobs in those early years — including teacher, domestic servant, and Civil War nurse — writing was clearly her passion.

In 1854, under the pen name of Flora Fairfield, she published her first story, "The Rival Prima Donnas," in Boston's *Saturday Evening Gazette*. The same year, James T. Fields read her essay "How I Went Out to Service" and suggested she abandon writing and "stick to . . . teaching." Nevertheless Louisa persisted, constantly writing

in a number of genres — from theatrical drama, poems, and love stories to gothic mysteries and blood-and-thunder tales. Her short pieces were soon followed by books, including *Flower Fables* (1854) — written for Emerson's daughter and inspired on walks with Thoreau — and *Hospital Sketches* (1863), which described her nursing experiences during the Civil War.

It was here in Orchard House that Louisa wrote many of her short stories for popular journals, including the *Atlantic Monthly* and far less memorable "juveniles." Yet the house will always be remembered as the fictional setting for *Little Women* (1868), her blockbuster novel that cast the four Alcott daughters as Meg, Jo, Beth, and Amy in the retelling of their family experiences. Orchard House is also where Louisa actually wrote *Little Women:*

> *"Jo! Jo, where are you?" cried Meg, at the foot of the garret stairs.*
> *"Here!!" answered a husky voice from above; and, running up, Meg found her sister eating apples and crying over the* Heir of Redclyffe, *wrapped up in a comforter on an old three-legged sofa by the sunny window. This was Jo's favorite refuge; and here she loved to retire with a half a dozen russets and a nice book to enjoy the quiet and the society of a pet rat who lived near by, and didn't mind her a particle.*

Visitors to Orchard House will recognize and appreciate many rooms, objects, and the aura described in *Little Women,* including bedchambers, kitchen, study, and parlor as well as May's drawings on her walls, a trunk of theatrical costumes, and Louisa's

Little Women, first edition frontispiece, 1858, with illustration by May Alcott

half-moon desk and inkwell. The dining room looks much as it did when the Alcotts and their guests, many of them writers and intellectuals, were entertained here by music, theater, and good conversation.

It's interesting to note that many of the March family adventures did not actually take place here at Orchard House, for Alcott liberally incorporated segments of many of her former homes into *Little Women.* (In the course of their marriage, her parents lived in more than twenty different places!) In fact, many of the childhood events she describes occurred at the Alcotts' former home Hillside — the house Hawthorne called Wayside — right next door.

Though Louisa and Bronson have garnered most of the press over the years, every member of the family was interested in writing, from journals, letters, and poems to books and plays. Anna was particularly fond of acting and joined the Concord Dramatic Union, Elizabeth was a gifted musician who died when she was twenty-two, and May — whose early students included the young Daniel Chester French — became a professional artist, though her career was ended by her untimely death at the age of thirty-nine.

French later remembered the Alcotts and their home in Caroline Ticknor's *May Alcott, A Memoir*

(1927): *I was always included . . . in the frequent invitations to supper or evening gatherings [at Orchard House] where there were literary games of charades or only conversation. Serene and courtly, his long silver locks curling about his neck, his fresh pink and white complexion set off by an expanse of snowy linen with white cravat, Mr. Alcott had much the aspect of an old portrait. He looked on at our diversions as from a loftier sphere, occasionally joining in the conversation or smiling approvingly at the humor of it, while the dear old lady who had not only been his helpmeet, but also a mainstay to the erratic genius through the many anxious years before the talented Louisa came so*

AUTHOR / AUTHOR !

Gish Jen on Louisa May Alcott and Ralph Waldo Emerson

I was Jo March, of course — writing away, cutting my hair, ever so gently refusing rich Teddy. Is there a woman writer in America who would not say so? How she loved Marmee, and indulged Amy, but chose for herself the most unglamorous Professor Bhaer? And who would not return, if she could, to the clear-cut world of the March family, worldly privations and all — to that warmth and nobility and simplicity?

I suspect I took the pen name Gish Jen in part because it sounded like Jo March — an androgynous spondee that spoke of independence. I invented myself in her image, and if one day I had to leave her and her author behind — if I had to progress beyond *Pilgrim's Progress,* and "drying tears and bearing burdens" — it was not without a heartache much like that with which Jo left her first family and first self.

As for where I ventured — that was first of all down the street to tangle, like Margaret Fuller, with Emerson. Was there ever a thinker more at odds with Confucius? Self-reliance! What an idea. For anyone Emerson threatens to burn down the house; for this nice Chinese girl he seemed to torch the whole countryside. And yet his call, not only for a new literature, but for a literature endlessly new, for writers who write not only against the past but against their own best inventions — that seemed a call I could hear. There was room in his program for me, for anyone; anyone could be an American writer, she only had to find her power, then find it again; to name herself Man Thinking.

Emerson was the first subversive, and still inspires every serious writer. The goal is still to gather up our times' rejected thoughts, and to return them, if we can, with a certain alienated majesty.

gallantly to the rescue, lent to the conversation her sweet reasonableness and her ever-quick response. The daughters, however, were most in evidence, as their elders seemed to wish. Miss Louisa's nimble wit and Miss May's gayety were sure to make material for diversion. One felt here that indeed "people were of more importance than things."

In the same memoir, French fondly remembered May Alcott as his first art mentor: *I may be able to record the peculiar debt I owe her in introducing me to the potentialities of sculpture. I had been whittling and carving things from wood and gypsum, and even from turnips, as many boys do, and, as usual, "the family" thought the product remarkable. My father spoke about them to Miss Alcott, as the artist of the community, and she, with her ever-ready enthusiasm, immediately offered to give me her modeling clay and tools. . . . I still [half a century later] have one of the modeling tools she gave me.*

Like The Wayside, Orchard House was preserved at the turn of the twentieth century by **Margaret Sidney** — the pen name of **Harriett Mulford Stone Lothrop** — who promoted the cause of historic preservation in Concord. In addition to saving Orchard House and The Wayside, she preserved the Grapevine Cottage (the home of the famed Concord grape) and the Old Tolman House on Monument Square. Though she wrote books on Concord's rich history, Lothrop was best remembered for her popular adventures of a family of five mischievous siblings known as "the Little Peppers." The best-known volume of this children's series, *Five Little Peppers and How They Grew* (1881), sold more than two million copies in its first fifty years.

Drive back on Lexington Road toward the center of Concord. On the right you'll see the beautiful home of the **Concord Art Association**, which was once used as a safe house for escaped slaves on the Underground Railroad.

On the left, the First Parish Church stands on the site of the Provincial Congress meetings of 1774–1775, which resolved to stockpile military supplies in Concord and raise companies of minute men in the neighboring villages. Just beyond the church is the old **Wright Tavern**, where the British regulars assembled in April 1775 before proceeding to the North Bridge.

Bear to the right, passing through **Monument Square** and past the town's prominent Civil War memorial. (When the memorial was dedicated in 1867, Ralph Waldo Emerson was asked to give the speech.) Across the street is the **Concord Town House**, which served not only as Town Hall but also as a popular lecture hall and rallying point for writers, abolitionists, and other prominent figures in the nineteenth century, from Emerson, Thoreau, and Bronson Alcott to William Lloyd Garrison, Wendell Phillips, and John Brown.

In April 1875, President Ulysses S. Grant and other government officials commemorated the centennial of the Revolution in Concord. A group of women gathered here, at the Town House, awaiting the escort that had been promised them to the festivities at the North Bridge. Curiously, no one came. Louisa May Alcott remembered the ladies' furor later that year in an article for the *Woman's Journal: Patience has its limits, and . . . when some impetuous soul cried out "Come on and let us take care of ourselves" . . . skirts were kilted up, arms locked, and with one accord, the light brigade charged over the red bridge, up the hill, into the tented field, rosy and red-nosed, dishevelled but dauntless. . . . [Be warned that the] tax-paying women of Concord, will not be left to wait uncalled upon . . . and, following in the footsteps of their forefathers, will utter another protest that shall be heard "round the world."*

It's probably no surprise that in 1880, Louisa, an ardent supporter of woman's suffrage, became the first woman to vote here in a local school election. It should be no surprise either that Concord's residents vote in this same Town Hall today.

Sleepy Hollow Cemetery

APPROXIMATE TIME: 45–60 MINUTES

Turn right just before Town Hall onto Route 62 East. The winding country road — a mere three tenths of a mile from Town Hall — leads to the main entrance of **Sleepy Hollow Cemetery**, which shares its name with Washington Irving's popular novel.

Following in the innovative footsteps of Mount Auburn Cemetery (1831) in Cambridge, Sleepy Hollow was designed as a beautifully landscaped rural garden cemetery. As at Mount Auburn, the land here was already a popular wooded walking place frequented by Hawthorne, Fuller, Emerson, and their friends. Interestingly, Henry David Thoreau was hired to survey Sleepy Hollow's pond and the road that leads to the front gate. And it was Ralph Waldo Emerson — Concord's acknowledged spiritual center and perennial orator of choice — who was asked to give the address at the cemetery's formal consecration in 1855.

"Shadows haunt these groves," Emerson observed in his speech. "All that ever lived about them clings to them.... And when these acorns that are falling at our feet are oaks overshadowing our children in a remote century, this mute green bank will be full of history."

The "mute green bank" filled with the most literary history at Sleepy Hollow is called **Authors Ridge**, clearly marked by signs inside the cemetery. Hawthorne, Thoreau, Emerson, the Alcotts, and Margaret Sidney are interred on this hill. Elizabeth Peabody, of bookshop fame, is another resident; her gravesite is below Authors Ridge.

In its earliest days, Sleepy Hollow was a relatively undiscovered gem — or so thought Nathaniel Hawthorne, as noted in his *Passages from the American Notebooks* (1868): *After leaving the book at Mr. Emerson's, I returned through the woods, and entering Sleepy Hollow, I perceived a lady reclining near the path which bends along its verge. It was Margaret herself. She had been there the whole afternoon, meditating or reading.... She said that nobody had broken her solitude, and was just giving utterance to a theory that no inhabi-*

tant of Concord ever visited Sleepy Hollow, when we saw a whole group of people entering the sacred precincts. . . . In the midst of our talk we heard footsteps above us, on the high bank: and while the intruder was still hidden among the trees, he called to Margaret, of whom he had gotten a glimpse. Then he emerged from the green shade; and, behold, it was Mr. Emerson, who, in spite of his clerical consecration, had found no better way of spending the Sabbath than to ramble among the woods. He appeared to have had a pleasant time; for he said that there were Muses in the woods today, and whispers to be heard in the breezes.

The beloved Hawthorne, at the age of sixty, was one of the first of his illustrious circle to die. He was buried at Sleepy Hollow in 1864, only nine years after it had been consecrated. James T. Fields remembered that bittersweet day in *Yesterdays With Authors* (1871): *On the 24th of May we carried Hawthorne through the blossoming orchards of Concord, and laid him down under a group of pines, on a hillside, overlooking historic fields. All the way from the village church to the grave the birds kept up a perpetual melody. The sun shone brightly, and the air was sweet and pleasant, as if death had never entered the world. Longfellow and Emerson, Channing and Hoar, Agassiz and Lowell, Greene and Whipple, Alcott and Clarke, Holmes and Hillard, and other friends whom he loved, walked slowly by his side that beautiful spring morning. The companion of his youth and his manhood, for whom he would willingly, at any time, have given up his own life, Franklin Pierce, was there among the rest, and scattered flowers into the grave. The unfinished Romance, which had cost him so much anxiety, the last literary work on which he had ever been engaged, was laid on his coffin.*

Not surprisingly, the Literary Trail's omnipresent sculptor, **Daniel Chester French** (1850–1931), has a major piece at Sleepy Hollow. The moving Melvin Memorial (1906–1908) honors three brothers — Asa, John, and Samuel Melvin — all of whom joined the First Massachusetts Heavy Artillery, Company K, and were killed in the Civil War. Like the Milmore Memorial, which French created for two brothers at Forest Hills Cemetery, the Melvin features a majestic female angel draped in a shroud and holding a bouquet. While Forest Hills's *Death and the Sculptor* shows the maternal, loving angel of death facing the artist while gently stopping his hand, the Melvin angel faces forward, sensually peering out from beneath the heavy drape. And while the former is cast in bronze, the latter is a marble rendering.

Though French was born in Exeter, New Hampshire, his family moved to Cambridge, Massachusetts, before settling permanently in Concord. His mother reportedly noticed little "Dan's" potential as a sculptor when the child began making comic characters from her turnips. Since Boston had no school of sculpture at the time, Dan picked up some principles of art from May Alcott, who had returned from her art studies in Paris. Other early inspiration came from William Morris Hunt, John Quincy Adams Ward, and William Rimmer.

Daniel Chester French, *Minute Man*

French's break came through his friend Ralph Waldo Emerson, who helped him win his first major commission; the *Minute Man* was unveiled for the centennial celebration at the North Bridge in Concord on April 19, 1875. After traveling in Europe, gathering knowledge and inspiration from different studios, French returned to the United States, where he worked, studied, and developed his distinctive style.

By 1913, when he received the commission for the Lincoln Memorial in Washington, D.C., French was considered America's leading sculptor. He died in 1931, at Chesterwood, his summer studio in the Berkshire hills of western Massachusetts. He maintained a home and studio in Concord, now privately owned, throughout his life.

Return to Monument Street on Route 62 West. Turn right and follow the road down to the parking lot by the North Bridge.

The Old Manse, at 269 Monument Street, is another example of the intertwining revolutions in Concord. The Reverend William Emerson, a patriot minister, built the house in 1770. He responded to and later wrote in his journal about the alarm of April 19, 1775, and the historic encounter on the North Bridge. Six decades later, his grandson Ralph Waldo Emerson began writing *Nature* from his second-floor study here, overlooking the site of the North Bridge. While boarding at The Old Manse, Emerson was asked to deliver an address on the bicentennial of the town of Concord. He delivered his "Historical Discourse," which borrowed from Grandfather Emerson's Patriot journals, on September 11, 1835, flanked by elderly survivors of the North Bridge encounter.

The young Nathaniel Hawthorne and his wife, Sophia Peabody, spent what they claimed were the "three happiest years" of their lives, from 1842 through 1844, when they rented The Old Manse. Of the seventeen short stories Hawthorne wrote here, sixteen were published in *Mosses from an Old Manse,* in which he immortalized this beloved home: *How gently, too, did the sight of the Old Manse — best seen from the river, overshadowed with its willows, and all environed about with the foliage of its orchard and avenue — how gently did its gray, homely aspect rebuke the spectacular extravagances of the day!*

Do note that it was Hawthorne, not the Emersons, who gave this structure its name. The word "manse" means the house of a clergyman, or a parsonage, and alluded to its builder and first inhabitant, the Reverend William Emerson.

Visitors can see the original structure and its minor additions as well as the vegetable garden — cultivated since the eighteenth century and planted in 1842 by

Old Manse, Concord, circa 1885

North Bridge, Concord

Thoreau as a wedding gift for the Hawthornes. The dining room window and the north window of the upstairs study bear a number of inscriptions from this time, etched with Sophia's diamond wedding ring. Hawthorne and Emerson's study — where, typically, Hawthorne faced in and Emerson faced out — is a revered site. So too is the **Concord River**, which flows behind The Old Manse, and which many an author delighted to describe.

Hawthorne, for example, mused on the river's peace and pace in *Mosses from an Old Manse: It may well be called the Concord, the river of peace and quietness; for it is certainly the most unexcitable and sluggish stream that ever loitered imperceptibly towards its eternity — the sea.*

Thoreau made a similar observation in *A Week on the Concord and Merrimack Rivers: [The] Concord River is remarkable for the gentleness of its current, which is scarcely perceptible, and some have referred to its influence on the proverbial moderation of the inhabitants of Concord, as exhibited in the Revolution and on later occasions. It has been proposed that the town should adopt for its coat of arms a field verdant, with the Concord circling nine times round. I have read the descent of an eighth of an inch in a mile is sufficient to produce a flow. Our river has, probably, very near the smallest allowance.*

You can see the serenely sluggish Concord River by walking past The Old Manse toward the **North Bridge**.

Though commonly called the Old North Bridge — and mislabeled as such on the sign in the Monument Street parking lot — this majestically rustic bridge was erected in 1956, replacing three other commemorative versions from 1875, 1889, and 1909.

The truly old North Bridge, where the "shots heard 'round the world" were fired in 1775, was deliberately dismantled by the town of Concord in 1793. Though romantic versions of the tale have the British regulars ripping up planks in anger and feeble defense, the truth is substantially tamer. (Yes, they yanked off a few boards but came nowhere near destroying the bridge.) After years of argument in town meeting, Concord acknowledged that populations had shifted and roads had been

---

AUTHOR / AUTHOR!

Jane Langton on "The Importance of Whiskers"

One of our librarian aunts must have given us a set of Authors cards. The suits were not hearts and diamonds, spades and clubs, but Ralph Waldo Emerson (no facial hair, gentle smile), Oliver Wendell Holmes (side-whiskers), Nathaniel Hawthorne (handlebar mustache), John Greenleaf Whittier (chin-whiskers), James Russell Lowell (short hair, bushy mustache, and whiskers), Henry Wadsworth Longfellow (the works).

It was a boring-looking set of cards. We didn't care. It was just a game, played cross-legged on the floor. My brother would ask for *The Autocrat of the Breakfast Table,* hoping to round out his Holmes suit, my sister wanted *The Village Blacksmith* to complete her set of Longfellow.

But — how extraordinary it seems now — Henry Thoreau was not part of the game. I suppose at that time he wasn't thought worthy of such select company. Now, of course, he has transcended all the rest.

It wasn't till many years later that those tiresome-looking old men became interesting to me, especially since they were so profoundly imbedded in the local landscape. Well, they're everywhere, these august presences. Their clever faces, their works, their Olympian friendships, all of these things provide a dense thicket for a mystery writer to wander in. Somehow they fatten and enrich a meagre plot.

Today I can't cross Boston Common without thinking of Emerson walking there with Walt Whitman — nor can I walk up Tremont Street without remembering the Saturday Club at the Parker House. I wish I knew in which Cambridgeport house Emily Dickinson spent many a homesick month while consulting a doctor about her eyes. Nor is it possible to find on Charles Street the house of publisher James Fields, where Dickens was an ailing guest in 1868, and where Annie Fields lived in a "Boston marriage" with Sarah Orne Jewett after her husband's death. Have you ever felt something tickle your cheek as you walk down Brattle Street? I'll tell you what it is — it's the ghostly whiskers of some long-dead transcendentalist.

realigned. So the obsolete North Bridge was replaced by a more conveniently located bridge a few hundred yards away.

The bridge here today is still a breathtaking sight; it is probably closer to the design of the original bridge than any that preceded it. On the Monument Street side is the obelisk memorializing one of the opening battles of the American Revolution, dedicated on July 4, 1837. It was for this ceremony that Emerson wrote his "Concord Hymn."

Across the river is French's impressive bronze *Minute Man* on a seven-foot granite pedestal. Cast in the Ames Foundry in Chicopee, Massachusetts, the statue was made from ten Civil War cannon donated to the project by Congress. Inscribed with the "Concord Hymn," the statue was dedicated — along with the 1875 version of the North Bridge — in the centennial festivities of April 19, 1775:

By the rude bridge that arched the flood,
Their flag to April's breeze unfurled,
Here once the embattled farmers stood,
And fired the shot heard 'round the world.

Return to **Concord Center** and Monument Square on Monument Street. You'll pass the **Colonial Inn**, the right section of which was once the home of Thoreau's aunts and housed his entire family during Henry's last two years of study at Harvard. The Colonial Inn is still a popular gathering place and a perfect place to stop for afternoon tea.

The brick **Masonic Lodge Building** on the next corner was a school where Thoreau taught after his graduation from college. He soon resigned from the job, refusing to use corporal punishment for his students.

Bearing left around the square, the site of the old **Concord Jail** is on your right. In July 1846, Thoreau spent the night here for refusing to pay his federal taxes. His protest was heard often: he was withholding funds from a government that condoned slavery and that engaged in a war he did not support. This experience led to his writing *Civil Disobedience* in 1849.

Turn right onto Main Street. Wending your way through the center of town, you'll see streets and buildings that would still look familiar to the Alcotts, Emersons, Thoreaus, and their friends. Though the names and owners have changed, the basic layout, many of the buildings, and the aura have not. Fine places for literary browsing include bookshops, new and used, as well as the library.

Main Street leads you to the **Concord Free Public Library**, a fine and architecturally fascinating building. Its collections include an astonishing number of books by

Concord's resident authors, both past and present, including rare first editions. In the library's rotunda is a seated statue of Emerson by Daniel Chester French.

If you stay on Main Street, forking to the right of the library, you will pass Academy Lane on the left. This is the neighborhood where Henry David Thoreau and his older brother John started their own coeducational high school, which lasted for three years. The building was later moved and can now be seen at 25 Middle Street, the first right turn off Academy.

Continue down Main Street toward the light at the intersection with Thoreau Street. Three houses before that light, on the left side of the street, is a yellow house numbered 255, the **Thoreau-Alcott house**. Thoreau lived here for the last dozen years of his life, from 1850 to 1862. In 1877, the year after America's Centennial celebration, Louisa May Alcott and her sister Anna (Jo and Meg of *Little Women*) bought this house. Their mother, called Marmee in the novel, died here in 1877.

Turn left at the lights onto Thoreau Street, which you will follow to Route 2 and Walden Pond. Just after turning onto Thoreau, note Belknap Street on the right. It leads to the neighborhood where the Thoreaus lived while Henry was at Walden Pond. He used to walk on the railroad tracks here,

since they provided the most direct route between this site and his Walden house.

As you continue on Thoreau Street, on the right you'll pass the old **Concord Depot** for the Fitchburg Railroad. The commuter rail from Boston makes regular stops here, as have thousands of trains since the Golden Age of American literature. The Fitchburg Railroad first stopped in Concord in June of 1844. Without it, Emerson *et al.* might have traveled far less frequently from Concord to Boston — and thereby been far less present at Ticknor & Fields, the Boston Athenaeum, Saturday Club meetings at the Parker House, and other favorite haunts.

In May 1873, the depot was the site of one particularly poignant and spectacular event. A year earlier, the Emerson home had been ruined by a major fire, forcing the family to travel to Europe while the house was repaired. On their return in 1873, the Emersons' train was greeted at the depot by an assemblage of Concord's finest citizens and a brass band playing "Home Sweet Home."

Then, as ever, Emerson appreciated his depot and train and the freedom they allowed. As he noted in "Culture," from *The Conduct of Life* (1860): *[T]he aesthetic value of railroads is to unite the advantages of town and country life, neither of which we can spare. A man should*

Henry David Thoreau's cabin on a title page of *Walden* (1854)

(1817–1862) built his 10-by-15-foot cabin by hand in 1845 as a place to escape the bustling outside world, to confront himself, and to "live deliberately."

A Harvard graduate, Thoreau was twenty-eight years old when he began his two years, two months, and two days at Walden, reading, writing, walking, and thinking in Spartan semi-solitude. Like his friend and mentor Ralph Waldo Emerson, who loaned him the land for the cabin, Thoreau believed the idealist transcendental philosophy that studying nature and knowing oneself were one and the same. *We must learn to reawaken and keep ourselves awake . . . by an infinite expectation of the dawn,* he later noted in *Walden* (1854).

Despite legends to the contrary, Thoreau was not a hermit during his stay at Walden. He welcomed visitors, walked into the center of Concord — a surprisingly easy jaunt — and earned money surveying, selling vegetables to neighbors, and lecturing. And, Thoreau wasn't the only writer inspired by these calm, wooded shores. Walden

live in or near a large town . . . In town he can find . . . opera, theater and panorama; the chemist's shop, the museum of natural history; the gallery of fine arts; the national orators, in their turn. . . . In the country he can find solitude and reading, manly labor, cheap living and his old shoes.

After crossing Route 2, you'll find yourself on Walden Street (Route 126). Not far down the road is a large parking lot on your left. Leave your car here, then cross the road to the main entrance of Walden Pond.

A favorite recreational, beach, and picnic area for more than a century, **Walden Pond State Reservation** is also a major literary shrine. Here **Henry David Thoreau**

> Our village life would stagnate if it were not for the unexplored forests and meadows that surround it.
>
> — Henry David Thoreau, *Walden* (1854)

has proved a source of words, wisdom, and ideas for many Concord authors, both then and now.

Today, you can leisurely walk to the isolated site of Thoreau's cabin and drop commemorative stones on the cairn that Bronson Alcott and Mary Adams began here in 1872. You can also visit a furnished replica of the cabin, conveniently placed in the parking lot (another replica stands outside the Concord Museum). The Thoreau Society bookstore by the parking lot is well worth a visit.

Though lovers of literature now generally associate Walden Pond with Thoreau, his contemporaries did not. Instead, the most famous man at Walden Pond in the 1840s was the "Ice King," Frederic Tudor, whose international export company cut huge blocks of ice from the winter waters here, transported them to Boston ports via the Fitchburg Railroad, then sailed them to countries with warmer climates in need of cooling.

Thoreau — who loved Indian philosophers and kept a Hindu text, *The Bhagavad Gita*, next to his bed — was thrilled that ice from Walden might well end up in India.

All things, of course, shall pass. So too did Thoreau's retreat by

> I went to the woods because I wished to live deliberately, to front only the essential facts of life, and see if I could not learn what it had to teach, and not, when I came to die, discover that I had not lived.
>
> — Henry David Thoreau, *Walden* (1854)

Walden Pond, which he ended in 1847. In *Walden*, he later observed: *Time is but the stream I go a-fishing in. I drink at it; but while I drink I see the sandy bottom and detect how shallow it is. Its thin current slides away, but eternity remains.*

Though his time there was over, the lessons he learned were indelible: *I learned this, at least, by my experiment: that if one advances confidently in the direction of his dreams, and endeavors to live the life which he has imagined, he will meet with a success unexpected in common hours.*

When you come to the end of this final leg of the Literary Trail, you'll return via Route 126 to Route 2. Take a right on Route 2 and follow it back to Cambridge, a drive of 20–30 minutes.

Afterthought

〜

As much as Ralph Waldo Emerson loved Concord, Boston, and Cambridge — and reveled in his trips between them — he'd have to admit that they were lacking in one major area: cafés. The European tradition of leisurely sipping coffee in a cozy, congenial atmosphere had simply not come to America during his lifetime. As Emerson noted in his *Journal* (1864): *A town in Europe is a place where you can go into a café at a certain hour of every day, buy . . . a cup of coffee, for six sous, & at that price, have the company of the wits, scholars, & gentlemen fond of conversation. That is a cheap & excellent club, which finds & leaves all parties on a good mutual footing.*

More than a century after Emerson's death, Greater Boston has finally caught up with European café society. In fact, end your visit in Harvard Square, with its numerous bookstores, cafés, and bookstore-cafés — the perfect finale to a day of following the footsteps of America's literary giants.

Meanwhile, city and neighborhood newspapers in Cambridge, Boston, and Concord all include listings for literary events today — from book signings, author readings, lectures, and panel discussions to poetry readings, poetry slams, story swaps, and other special events.

While Greater Boston's book fairs, readings, signings, and related activities draw authors from around the nation and the world, these events frequently feature local *literati* as well. Our rich array of contributors to "Author/Author!" — Anne Bernays, Julia Child, Henry Louis Gates, Jr., Gish Jen, Justin Kaplan, Jane Langton, David McCullough, and Robert Pinsky — all live and work nearby. And although Patricia Smith has now moved away, she, like the others, makes both formal and informal appearances in Boston.

Other nationally acclaimed writers in the area include the novelists James Carroll (*Mortal Friends; An American Requiem*), Christopher Tilghman (*Mason's Retreat; In a Father's Place*), and Arthur Golden (*Memoirs of a Geisha*) and the biographer Doris Kearns Goodwin (*No Ordinary*

Time: Franklin and Eleanor Roosevelt; The Fitzgeralds and the Kennedys).

The poet and playwright Derek Walcott (*Omeros; The Arkansas Testament*) lives and teaches in the Greater Boston area, as does the poet Seamus Heaney (*The Spirit Level; Death of a Naturalist*), the research psychiatrist Robert Coles (*Children of Crisis*), and Robert Brustein (*Reimagining American Theatre; The Theatre of Revolt*), the founding director of the Yale Repertory and American Repertory theaters.

Alice Hoffman (*Angel Landing; Turtle Moon*) is also a Greater Bostonian, as is the nature writer John Hanson Mitchell (*Walking Towards Walden; Ceremonial Time*) and Robert Parker, author of the celebrated Spenser detective series. Although the novelist John Updike (*Rabbit, Run; Bech: A Book*) makes his home in the northern suburbs of Boston, he has roots at Harvard.

The Calendar section of the Thursday *Boston Globe* is arguably the best single resource for finding activities in the area, which are listed by category and location. Check the listings under "Poetry and Prose," "Lectures," "Museums," and "Walks and Tours." Many bookstores in the three towns also have bulletin boards with notices of upcoming literary events. Another convenient way to learn about the vibrant literary scene in this area is on local Web sites. The Literary Trail itself can be accessed at www.lit-trail.org.

Suggested Readings

Numerous biographies of the individuals mentioned in this guidebook are available in bookstores and libraries. Below are volumes, some in print and some not, that include tales, facts, and quotations by and about many of Greater Boston's literary community.

Amory, Cleveland, *The Proper Bostonians* (New York: Dutton, 1947).

Barksdale, Richard, and Keneth Kinnamon, *Black Writers of America: A Comprehensive Anthology* (New York: Macmillan, 1972).

Beatty, Noëlle Blackmer, *Literary Byways of Boston & Cambridge* (Washington, D.C.: Starrhill Press, 1991).

Corbett, William, *Literary New England: A History and Guide* (Boston: Faber and Faber, 1993).

Fields, James T., *Yesterdays With Authors* (Boston: Houghton Mifflin, 1871).

History Project, The, *Improper Bostonians* (Boston: Beacon Press, 1998).

Howe, M. A. DeWolfe, *Memories of a Hostess* (Boston: Atlantic Monthly Press, 1922).

————, *Who Lived Here? A Baker's Dozen of Historic New England Houses and Their Occupants* (New York: Bramhall House, 1952).

Jacobs, Donald M., ed., *Courage and Conscience: Black & White Abolitionism in Boston* (Bloomington: Indiana University Press for the Boston Athenaeum, 1993).

Kaledin, Eugenia, *Literary Boston: Boston 200 Broadside Series* (Boston: Boston 200, 1975).

Kaplan, Justin, ed., *Bartlett's Familiar Quotations, Sixteenth Edition* (Boston: Little, Brown, 1992).

Kaufman, Polly Welts, Bonnie Hurd Smith, et al., *Boston Women's Heritage Trail: Four Centuries of Boston Women* (Boston: Boston Women's Heritage Trail, 1999).

Linscott, Robert N., ed., *State of Mind: A Boston Reader* (New York: Farrar, Straus, 1948).

O'Connell, Shaun, *Imagining Boston: A Literary Landscape* (Boston: Beacon Press, 1990).

Swift, Lindsay, *Literary Landmarks of Boston* (Boston: Houghton Mifflin, 1903).

Tryon, W. S., *Parnassus Corner: A Life of James T. Fields* (Boston: Houghton Mifflin, 1963).

Wilson, Susan, *Garden of Memories: A Guide to Historic Forest Hills* (Boston: Forest Hills Educational Trust, 1998).

————, *Sites and Insights: A Multicultural Guide to Fifty Historic Landmarks In and Around Boston* (Boston: Beacon Press, 1994).

Winslow, Helen M., *Literary Boston of To-Day* (Boston: L. C. Page, 1902).

Museums and Historic Sites on the Literary Trail of Greater Boston

～

Below is a list of museums and other historic sites open to the general public that are mentioned in *The Literary Trail of Greater Boston*. Every effort has been made to be sure this information is accurate at the time of publication.

BOSTON

Boston Athenaeum
10½ Beacon Street
617-227-0270
www.bostonathenaeum.org
Closed for renovations through 2001
Wheelchair accessible

Boston Common
Bounded by Tremont, Park, Beacon, Boylston, and Charles streets
617-227-8955, Friends of the Public Garden and Common
617-635-7384, Boston Park Rangers
Open year-round, seasonal guided tours available, free admission
Wheelchair accessible

Boston Public Garden
Bounded by Charles, Beacon, Arlington, and Boylston streets
617-227-8955, Friends of the Public Garden and Common
617-635-7384, Boston Park Rangers
Open year-round, seasonal guided tours available, free admission
Wheelchair accessible

Boston Public Library
700 Boylston Street
617-536-5400
www.bpl.org
Open year-round, guided tours available, free admission
Wheelchair accessible

Commonwealth Avenue Mall
Commonwealth Avenue, from Arlington Street to Kenmore Square
617-227-8955, Friends of the Public Garden and Common
617-635-7384, Boston Park Rangers
Open year-round, seasonal guided tours available, free admission
Wheelchair accessible

Forest Hills Cemetery
95 Forest Hills Avenue
Jamaica Plain
617-524-0128
Open year-round, free admission, some fees for special events and periodic guided walks
Wheelchair accessible

Gibson House
137 Beacon Street
617-267-6338
Open year-round, admission fee
No wheelchair access

Granary Burying Ground
83–115 Tremont Street
Open year-round, free admission
617-635-7384, Boston Park Rangers
Wheelchair accessible

King's Chapel
58 Tremont Street
617-227-2155
Open year-round, free admission, fees may be charged for special events
Wheelchair accessible

King's Chapel Burying Ground
58 Tremont Street
617-635-7384, Boston Park Rangers
Open year-round, free admission
Wheelchair accessible

Massachusetts Historical Society
(A research library open to the public)
1154 Boylston Street
617-536-1608
www.masshist.org
Library open year-round, free admission
Wheelchair accessible

Massachusetts State House
Beacon and Park streets
617-727-3676, tours and information
Open year-round, free admission
Wheelchair accessible

Museum of Afro American History
Abiel Smith School
African Meeting House (closed for renovation)
8 Smith Court
617-739-1200
Open year-round, suggested donation
www.afroammuseum.org
Wheelchair accessible after renovations

Nichols House Museum
55 Mount Vernon Street
617-227-6993
Open year-round except January, admission fee
No wheelchair access

Old Corner Bookstore building
(Boston Globe Store)
1 School Street
617-367-4000
www.globestore.boston.com
Open year-round, free admission
Wheelchair accessible

Old South Meeting House
310 Washington Street
617-482-6439

www.oldsouthmeetinghouse.org
Open year-round, admission fee
Wheelchair accessible

Omni Parker House
60 School Street
617-227-8600
www.omnihotels.com
Open year-round, free admission
Wheelchair accessible

Park Street Church
One Park Street
617-523-3383
www.parkstreet.org
Open seasonally, free admission
Wheelchair accessible

Park Street MBTA Station
Corner of Park and Tremont streets
617-722-3200, MBTA customer service
www.mbta.com
Open year-round, token required for entry
Wheelchair accessible

William Hickling Prescott House
55 Beacon Street
617-742-3190
Open seasonally, admission fee
No wheelchair access

Tremont Temple
88 Tremont Street
617-523-7320
Open year-round, free admission, fees may
    be charged for special performances
Wheelchair accessible

CAMBRIDGE

The Cambridge Center for Adult Education
Located in a former home of Margaret Fuller
    and The Blacksmith House
42 and 56 Brattle Street
617-547-6789
www.ccae.org
Open year-round, fees charged for classes
    and special programs
Wheelchair accessible

Club Passim
47 Palmer Street
617-492-7679
www.clubpassim.com
Open year-round, admission fee charged for
    performances
No wheelchair access

Harvard University
Harvard Events & Information Center
1350 Massachusetts Avenue
617-495-1573
www.info_center@harvard.edu
Open year-round, guided tours available,
    free admission
Wheelchair access to Harvard Yard; call for
    information on individual campus
    buildings

Longfellow National Historic Site
105 Brattle Street
617-876-4491
www.nps.gov/long
Closed for renovations through 2001; guid-
    ed walking tours of Cambridge available

Mount Auburn Cemetery
580 Mount Auburn Street
617-547-7105; 617-864-9646
Open year-round, free admission, fees for
    maps, special events, and guided walks
Mostly wheelchair accessible

CONCORD

Colonial Inn
48 Monument Square
978-369-9200
www.concordscolonialinn.com
Open year-round, free admission
Restaurant and first floor wheelchair acces-
    sible

Concord Free Public Library
129 Main Street
978-318-3300
www.mln.lib.ma.us
Open year-round, free admission
Wheelchair accessible

Concord Museum
200 Lexington Road (entrance on
    Cambridge Turnpike)
978-369-9763
www.concordmuseum.org
Open year-round, admission fee
Wheelchair accessible

Concord Town House
Town government offices for Concord
22 Monument Square
978-318-3001
Open year-round, free admission
Wheelchair accessible

Ralph Waldo Emerson House
28 Cambridge Turnpike
978-369-2236
Open seasonally, admission fee
No wheelchair access

North Bridge Site
Minute Man National Historical Park
Monument Street
978-369-6993
www.nps.gov/mima
Open year-round, free admission
Wheelchair accessible

The Old Manse
269 Monument Street
978-369-3909
www.thetrustees.org
Open seasonally, admission fee
First-floor wheelchair accessible

Orchard House
399 Lexington Road
978-369-4118
www.louisamayalcott.org
Open year-round except for first two weeks
    in January, admission fee
First floor wheelchair accessible

Sleepy Hollow Cemetery
Bedford Street (Route 62)
Open year-round, free admission
Partly wheelchair accessible (Authors Ridge
    is not accessible)

Walden Pond State Reservation
915 Walden Street (Route 126)
978-369-3254
www.magnet.state.ma.us/dem/parks/
wldn.htm
Open year-round, parking fee
Wheelchair accessible gift shop and bathrooms

The Wayside
455 Lexington Road
978-369-6993, 6975
www.nps.gov/mima/wayside
Open seasonally, admission fee
Wheelchair accessible Visitor Center

TRAILS

The following Trails can be self-guided or you can join a group tour. Call for further information.

Black Heritage Trail/Boston African
American National Historic Site
617-742-5415

Boston by Sea: A Musical Cruise Through
Boston's Past
Boston History Collaborative
617-227-4321
www.bostonharborcruises.com
www.bostonbysea.org

Boston Family History Web Site (Virtual
tour of Boston's ethnic neighborhoods)
Boston History Collaborative
617-574-5950
www.BostonFamilyHistory.com

Boston Women's Heritage Trail
617-522-2872, 617-576-3869
www.bwht.org

Freedom Trail
617-242-5642
www.thefreedomtrail.org

Literary Trail of Greater Boston
Boston History Collaborative
617-574-5950
www.lit-trail.org

Other Sites of Literary Interest

Site of Brook Farm
(Interpretive signage at site)
670 Baker Street
West Roxbury, Massachusetts
Open year-round, free admission

Fruitlands Museums
102 Prospect Hill Road
Harvard, Massachusetts
978-456-3924
www.fruitlands.org
Open seasonally, admission fee
Partially wheelchair accessible, call for
information

House of the Seven Gables
54 Turner Street
Salem, Massachusetts
978-744-0991
www.7gables.org
Open year-round except January 1–17,
admission fee
First floor, grounds, and museum shop
wheelchair accessible

John F. Kennedy Library and Museum
Columbia Point
Boston, Massachusetts
617-929-4523
www.cs.umb.edu/jfklibrary/
museum.htm
Open year-round, admission fee
Wheelchair accessible

Judith Sargent Murray House Museum
49 Middle Street
Gloucester, Massachusetts
978-281-2432
www.hurdsmith.com/judith
Open seasonally, admission fee
No wheelchair access

John Greenleaf Whittier Birthplace
305 Whittier Road
Haverhill, Massachusetts
978-373-3979
Open year-round, admission fee
No wheelchair access

Illustration Credits

The authors gratefully acknowledge permission to reproduce the following illustrations.

Copyrighted photographs by Susan Wilson: African Meeting House, Blacksmith House, Boston Athenaeum, Boston Public Library Grand Staircase, Forest Hills Cemetery, Margaret Fuller cenotaph, Samuel Eliot Morison statue, Mount Auburn Cemetery, Old South Meeting House, Public Garden, 54th Regiment Memorial, Elizabeth Pain tombstone, The Wayside

Courtesy of Susan Wilson: Pi Alley

Courtesy of the Boston Public Library Print Department: Henry Adams, e. e. cummings, Charles Dickens, Benjamin Franklin, Robert Frost, Martin Luther King, Jr., Robert Lowell, Eugene and Carlotta O'Neill, Francis Parkman, Edgar Allan Poe statue, Walt Whitman, Malcolm X, William Lloyd Garrison, *Last Hurrah* movie still

Courtesy of the Louisa May Alcott Memorial Association: Louisa May Alcott, Bronson Alcott, Little Women frontispiece

Courtesy of the Schlesinger Library, Radcliffe Institute, Harvard University: Lydia Maria Child, Frederick Douglass, Fannie Farmer, Margaret Fuller, Helen Keller with Annie Sullivan and Edward Everett Hale, Sara Josepha Hale, Thomas Wentworth Higginson, Julia Ward Howe, William James, Sarah Orne Jewett, Elizabeth Peabody, Anne Sexton, Lucy Stone, Harriet Beecher Stowe, John Updike, Phillis Wheatley, John Greenleaf Whittier, "Beacon Street," Boston Common and Massachusetts State House, Louisburg Square, Radcliffe Yard

Courtesy of Harvard University: W.E.B. Du Bois, Harvard Yard, John Harvard statue, Houghton Library, Memorial Hall, Widener Library (Rose Lincoln photograph)

Courtesy of the Boston Athenaeum: Annie Adams Fields (Gift of Mrs. E. Sturgis Hinds), Henry James, Amy Lowell, Cotton Mather, *The Liberator*, Newspaper Row

Courtesy of Houghton Mifflin Company: James T. Field with Nathaniel Hawthorne and George Ticknor, Oliver Wendell Holmes, Sr., James Russell Lowell, Old Corner Bookstore

Courtesy of Kahlil and Jean Gibran, © 1974: Kahlil Gibran, c. 1910

Courtesy of the National Park Service, Longfellow National Historic Site: Nathaniel Hawthorne, Longfellow House

Courtesy of the Concord Museum, Concord, MA: Central Concord, Title page of *Walden*

Courtesy of the Concord Museum and the R. W. Emerson Memorial Association: Emerson's study (Nanlee Smith photograph)

Courtesy of Minute Man National Historical Park, Concord, Massachusetts: Daniel Chester French's Minute Man, North Bridge

Courtesy of The Old Manse, a property of The Trustees of Reservations: Old Manse

Courtesy of Omni Parker House: Parker House

Author/Author! Contributors

Anne Bernays is the author of *Growing Up Rich, Professor Romeo,* and six other novels. She is a co-author of two books of nonfiction and many essays and book reviews. Long a teacher of writing, Bernays is currently working on a double memoir, with Justin Kaplan, on New York in the 1950s.

Julia Child has introduced millions of Americans to the art of French cooking with her lively television broadcasts and cookbooks. She settled in Cambridge, Massachusetts, shortly after the publication of her first cookbook, *Mastering the Art of French Cooking.* In the four decades since, she has won two Emmy awards for her television programs and her books have appeared on best-seller lists across the country.

Henry Louis Gates, Jr., one of *Time* magazine's "25 Most Influential Americans," is the chair of Afro-American Studies and director of the W.E.B. Du Bois Institute at Harvard University. He has written several books of literary criticism and is the editor of anthologies, encyclopedias, and magazines on the black experience. His numerous awards include a grant from the MacArthur Foundation and election to the Academy of Arts and Letters.

Gish Jen has written two notable novels, *Typical American* and *Mona in the Promised Land,* and a collection of stories, *Who's Irish?* A graduate of Harvard University and the recipient of grants from the Bunting Institute, the Guggenheim Foundation, and the National Endowment for the Arts, among others, she lives in Cambridge, Massachusetts, with her husband and two children.

Justin Kaplan, general editor of the sixteenth and seventeenth editions of *Bartlett's Familiar Quotations,* is the author of several biographies, including the Pulitzer Prize–winning *Mr. Clemens and Mark Twain* as well as *The Language of Names* (with Anne Bernays). He and his wife, Anne Bernays, live in Cambridge and are collaborating on a book about New York in the 1950s.

Jane Langton has written fourteen suspense novels, including *The Memorial Hall Murder, The Transcendental Murder,* and *Emily Dickinson Is Dead.* Her Homer and Mary Kelly mysteries have been praised by the *New York Times Book Review* for their "evocative and loving use" of Greater Boston locales. She lives in Lincoln, Massachusetts.

David McCullough is well known to TV audiences as the host of *The American Experience* and the narrator of numerous documentaries, including *The Civil War*. Winner of the Pulitzer Prize, the Francis Parkman Prize, the National Book Award, and other honors, McCullough has written a number of histories, including *The Johnstown Flood, The Great Bridge, Brave Companions,* and *Truman*. He lives with his wife, Rosalee Barnes McCullough, in West Tisbury, Massachusetts.

Robert Pinsky, the thirty-ninth Poet Laureate of the United States, has written numerous books of poetry and prose. He has also trans-lated the *Inferno* of Dante and has been the poetry editor of the Internet magazine *Slate*. Pinsky teaches in the graduate writing program at Boston University and lives with his wife, Ellen, in Newton, Massachusetts.

Patricia Smith, a former columnist for the *Boston Globe* and a four-time National Poetry Slam champion, is the author of *Africans in America*, the companion book to PBS's groundbreaking series, and the poetry volumes *Life According to Motown, Big Towns, Big Talk,* and *Close to Death*. Now a columnist for *Ms. Magazine*, Smith is working on her first novel.

Index